The Forsaken Crusade

DEDICATION

With love to Bill,
my father

Always there for all of us

THE FORSAKEN CRUSADE

SIGMUND BROUWER

VICTOR BOOKS

A DIVISION OF SCRIPTURE PRESS PUBLICATIONS INC.
USA CANADA ENGLAND

THE WINDS OF LIGHT SERIES
Wings of an Angel
Barbarians from the Isle
Legend of Burning Water
The Forsaken Crusade

Cover design by Mardelle Ayres
Cover illustration by Jeff Haynie
Photo by Dwight Arthur

Library of Congress Cataloging-in-Publication Data

Brouwer, Sigmund, 1959—
   The forsaken crusade / by Sigmund Brouwer.
      p.   cm.—(The Winds of light series ; 4)
   Summary: In the early fourteenth century, the boy warrior Thomas
and his allies continue their efforts to regain the earldom of Magnus
from the false sorcerer Druids, who have taken control of it and now
threaten to conquer all of England.
   ISBN 0-89693-118-8
   [1. Druids and druidism—Fiction. 2. Knights and knighthood—
Fiction. 3. Christian life—Fiction. 4. England—Fiction.] I. Title.
II. Series: Brouwer, Sigmund, 1959- Winds of light series ; #4.
PZ7.B79984Fo 1992   92-15430
[Fic]—dc20   CIP
                                                AC

1 2 3 4 5 6 7 8 9 10 Printing/Year 96 95 94 93 92

VICTOR BOOKS
A division of SP Publications, Inc.
Wheaton, Illinois 60187

AUTHOR'S NOTE

For two thousand years—far north and east of London—the ancient English towns of Pickering, Thirsk, and Helmsley, and their castles, have guarded a line on the lowland plains between the larger centers of Scarborough and York.

In the beginning, Scarborough, with its high North Sea cliffs, was a Roman signal post. From there, sentries could easily see approaching barbarian ships, and were able to relay messages from Pickering to Helmsley to Thirsk, the entire fifty miles inland to the boundary outpost of York, where other troops waited—always ready—for any inland invasions.

When their empire fell, the Romans in England succumbed to the Anglo-Saxons, great savage brutes in tribal units who conquered as warriors, and over the generations became farmers. The Anglo-Saxons in turn, suffered defeat by raiding Vikings, who in turn lost to the Norman knights from France with their thundering war horses.

Through those hundreds and hundreds of years, that line from Scarborough to York never diminished in importance.

Some of England's greatest and richest abbeys—religious re-treats for monks—accumulated their wealth on the lowland plains along that line. Rievaulx Abbey, just outside Helmsley, contained 250 monks and owned vast estates of land which held over 13,000 sheep.

But directly north, lay the moors.

No towns or abbeys tamed the moors, which reached east hundreds of square miles to the craggy cliffs of the cold gray North Sea.

Each treeless and windswept moor plunged into deep divid-ing valleys of lush greenness that only made the heather-cov-ered heights appear more harsh. The ancients called these North York moors "Blackamoor."

Thus, in the medieval age of chivalry, 250 years after the Norman knights had toppled the English throne, this remote-ness and isolation protected Blackamoor's earldom of Magnus from the prying eyes of King Edward II and the rest of his royal court in London.

Magnus, as a kingdom within a kingdom, was small in com-parison to the properties of England's greater earls. This small-ness too was protection. Hard to reach and easy to defend, British and Scottish kings chose to overlook it, and in practical terms, it had as much independence as a separate country.

Magnus still had size, however. Its castle commanded and protected a large village and many vast moors. Each valley be-tween the moors averaged a full day's travel by foot. Atop the moors, great flocks of sheep grazed on the tender green shoots of heather. The valley interiors supported cattle and cultivated plots of land, farmed by peasants nearly made slaves by the yearly tribute exacted from their crops. In short, with sheep and wool and cattle and land, Magnus was not a poor earldom, and well worth ruling.

The entire story of Magnus is difficult to relate in a single volume. This volume, *The Forsaken Crusade*, follows three portions of its tale which have related how the orphan boy Thomas—then 14 and in those times old enough to be considered a man—conquered Magnus and released its village from murderous oppression. (That part of the tale is told in *Wings of an Angel*.)

Yet, along with power, a lordship has its responsibilities. Thomas must protect his people, and the second volume of the story of Magnus (*Barbarians from the Isle*) tells how Thomas battled the powerful northern Scots, then faced a far greater trial, one imposed by Druid false sorcerers who demanded he join their secret group, or lose his lordship and castle.

A victory against those Druids enabled Thomas to keep Magnus, but as the third volume (*Legend of Burning Water*) reveals, his victory was only temporary. Posing as false priests, the Druids regained Magnus; Thomas was forced to flee and take desperate action, guided by strangers he dared not trust, strangers who knew all of the truth behind Magnus.

As *The Forsaken Crusade* begins, Thomas holds ransom what he believes is his single last chance to regain Magnus. Unknown to him, the unseen strangers are equally desperate and must take action of their own.

Those interested in ancient times should know that Magnus itself cannot be found in any history book. Nor can Thomas be found. Nor his nurse Sarah, the wandering knight Sir William, Katherine, Geoffrey the Candlemaker, Tiny John, nor others of the collection of friends and foes of Thomas. Yet many of the more famous people and events found throughout its story shaped the times of that world, as historians may easily confirm.

KATHERINE
The Betrayal

LATE SPRING A. D. 1313

"Our friend Thomas is free," the old man said. "Yet, there is much that troubles me."

The girl almost woman beside him turned her face to watch his wrinkled features closely. *There is much that troubles me too. I cannot shake my last vision of him. The reins in his hands. The stallion in full flight. And her . . . far too beautiful, and holding Thomas far too tight behind him on that horse.*

Katherine did not voice those thoughts. Instead, she said simply, "I am sorry you are troubled."

They stood at the crossroads outside the town walls of York. Behind them, in York, lay the confusion and chaos of an entire population buzzing with the incredible news. *The lord's daughter has been taken hostage! Kidnapped in daylight beneath the very noses of the courtyard knights!*

Those same knights had already scattered in all directions from the crossroads where the old man and Katherine and a handful of travelers now stood, each knight engaged in useless pursuit of a powerful horse long since gone on roads which would carry no tracks.

One of the nearby travelers pausing at the busy crossroads might have found the picture of the old man and Katherine bent in conversation together to be warmly touching.

Katherine shone with the innocent loveliness given only to those who pay little heed to their own beauty. Her long blond hair was tightly braided. And, pulled back as it was from her face, it only showed more fully the smoothness of her soft skin, and the deep blue of eyes which seemed luminously aware of every detail around her.

She stood nearly as tall as the old man beside her, and when she leaned forward to listen to his quiet words, it was with a gentle grace that promised much for the woman she would mature to become.

The old man, however, would not have seemed exceptional to that same traveler. Despite the warm spring afternoon, the old man was draped in a loose black cloak that left exposed only his hands and sandaled feet. He was not a tall man. Indeed, with the stoop that forced him to lean heavily on the cane, his height had dropped to match that of the 15-year-old girl beside him.

Yet, had that traveler been able to see into the shadows cast over the man's face by his hood, he would have been met by a fierceness of eyes that burned with strength. Had that traveler taken away the old man's cane, he would have seen the stoop disappear, and found no shakes or trembles in the old man's gnarled hands. And had that traveler stolen the old man's cloak, he would have been amazed at its weight and the objects hidden inside.

Katherine and the old man, of course, paid little heed to any stranger's glance and, with much greater matters of concern, would have cared nothing of that stranger's impressions of their conversation.

The old man, in fact, had his head bent even lower now as he searched the hard ground of the well-traveled roads.

"Stay with me," he said softly. "We shall talk as we follow Thomas."

"Follow Thomas?" Katherine echoed with equal softness. "Half an army runs in circles of useless pursuit. If he has escaped them, most surely he has also escaped us."

The old man laughed quietly. "Hardly, my child. Do you not remember the puppy he left behind with his secret treasure of books?"

Of course. In the excitement of his escape, Katherine had allowed herself to forget that Thomas must soon return to the cave which held those books.

"Yes," she said quickly. "We shall find him there. We know he'll have to get back to his books within several days. After all, regardless of his plans, he will not let the puppy die there of starvation."

The old man continued his low chuckle. "That only demonstrates that once again when you think of Thomas, you think with your heart. You wish him to have the nobleness of mind that would not let an innocent animal die a horrible death."

"It is otherwise?" Katherine challenged, even though her face flushed at the old man's remark.

"Perhaps not. But others might believe Thomas will return to his puppy merely because of the more valuable books nearby."

Katherine ignored that. "So we proceed back to the valley of the cave and wait."

"Not so," the old man replied. "That is far too long, and time is now too precious."

"Until then?" Katherine asked. She did not want to think about the days which Thomas would pass in the company of such an attractive hostage, one who had once claimed a true love for Thomas.

"We will find Thomas by nightfall," the old man promised.

His head was still down, and he still examined the ground carefully.

"That shows much confidence."

"No," the old man smiled. "Forethought."

The old man grinned in triumph and then hurried ahead on the road which led east to Scarborough on the North Sea. Neither found it unusual that several of the strangers behind them followed the same road.

Several minutes later, the old man stopped and dropped his voice to a whisper.

"Speak truth now," he warned. "An hour back, in York, you were convinced I had lost my mind to purchase that sack of flour in the midst of our hurry to reach Thomas in the lord's courtyard before he could attempt to take his hostage."

Katherine hummed a noncommittal comment.

"Answer enough."

The old man tapped the ground at his feet with the end of his cane.

"There," he said. "Our trail to Thomas."

He rubbed the tip of his cane through a slight dusting of coarse unmilled flour.

Katherine nodded, unable to hide her own sudden smile at the old man's obvious delight in himself and at the implications of that flour. After all, in the courtyard had she not distracted the keeper of Thomas' horse while the old man loaded that flour into a saddlebag?

"Yes," the old man said as if reading her mind, "I cut a small hole in his saddle bag, and of course, in the sack of flour. Unmilled and still coarse, the flour that falls through is heavy enough to leave a trail wherever he goes."

2

A mile farther, Katherine remembered the old man's words at the crossroads.

"What troubles you about the freedom Thomas so dangerously earned?" she asked.

The old man's eyes searched ahead for the next traces of flour as he walked. He answered without pausing in his search.

"Thomas should never have escaped York."

"God was with him, to be sure," Katherine agreed.

"Perhaps," the old man said a step later, "but I suspect instead the Druids in York provided earthly help."

"He nearly lost his life," Katherine protested.

"Are you certain? Describe the events you recall."

Were not the subject matter so serious, Katherine might have enjoyed this test of logic. Somewhere in those events were clues the old man had noticed, and now wanted her to find.

She summoned vivid memories.

"He left the castle with Isabelle, a dagger hidden beneath his cloak and pressed against her ribs."

"Before that," the old man said with a trace of impatience.

"A boy watched his horse at the side of the courtyard."

"Katherine . . . " Now his voice held ominous warning.

Suddenly, she understood. And understanding brought a pain, as if her heart had twisted in her chest.

"On his arrival," Katherine said slowly, "he met with the Earl of York. A spy—named Waleran—in the neighboring cell overheard their entire conversation. That spy then hurried away as I entered the prison."

"Continue," the old man said. Satisfaction in her perception had replaced his rumblings of vexation.

"Much time passed as the Earl of York told me what Thomas intended," Katherine said. "Enough time for the spy Waleran to reach the castle and provide warning."

Katherine's heart twisted more at the implication.

With that much warning, how had Thomas succeeded? Unless those at the castle had not feared his actions. Unless he were one of them.

Another memory flashed. Of a knight blocking escape, with his huge broadsword raised high to cleave Thomas dead as the horse and its two riders galloped toward him. Until a stray arrow slammed through the knight's shoulder.

"It was no accident then," she said slowly, "that those arrows missed Thomas and instead struck the one knight able to stop him."

"Nor," the old man added, "that the drawbridge was not raised enough to hold him inside the town. Then raised high enough to keep the knights from immediate pursuit."

"Yet why?" Katherine moaned. Her words, however, were only meant as release for the sorrow which gripped her. She already knew the answer.

"Our much-used argument," the old man said. "The unseen Druid masters play a terrible and mysterious game of chess. Thomas belonged to us at birth. Too soon, we had no choice but to leave him among them, alone and only armed with those few books of knowledge. But many years have passed. Have the Druids claimed him as their own?"

"I've always said it could not be," Katherine murmured. "I could not argue with my heart. But this contrived escape. . . . "

The old man stopped and touched her arm in sympathy. It was a touch as light as the breeze which followed them down the road.

"Against the Druids, nothing is what it appears to be," the old man said. "They know we watch, even if they know not who we are. The more it would seem Thomas is not one of them, the more likely we might finally tell him the truth."

"And by telling him the truth behind Magnus," Katherine finished, "we shall arm them with what they so desperately seek. And in so doing lose a battle centuries old."

They walked farther in silence.

"What shall we do?" Katherine despaired.

"We shall play this mysterious chess game to the end," the old man said grimly. "We shall tell Thomas enough for him to believe we have been deceived. And arrange a surprise of our own. He shall soon be a pawn which belongs to us."

3

That night, Katherine paused in the edge of darkness just out-side the glow of light given by the flickers of a small fire in front of Thomas and his captive.

Thomas had chosen his camp wisely. He was flanked on two sides by walls of jagged rock; he was afforded protection, yet not trapped. The light of his fire was low enough that intruders passing even within twenty yards would not notice, and his horse—tethered to a nearby tree—had been muzzled so it could not betray them with noise.

Katherine had prepared herself to remain cold of heart for this moment. She had told herself again and again since leaving York that she would not care how Thomas had chosen to react to his hostage. What would it matter if she would step into the firelight and find the two gathered together side by side to seek warmth against the night chill, Isabelle's long hair soft against Thomas' face as she leaned on his shoulder?

It would matter, Katherine discovered as her heart seemed to soar upward when she surveyed their makeshift camp. For they were not together, and much as she was forced to suspect Thomas was one of the false sorcerer Druids, it filled her with relief to discover the pair far apart.

Thomas was seated on a log, leaning with two hands on the hilt of a sword propped point first into the ground, and staring into the flames. He seemed oblivious of Isabelle on her blanket at the side of the fire. Moreover, Isabelle's hands were tied together and her feet hobbled no less differently than might have been done to a common donkey.

Hardly the signs of romance!

Katherine smiled, then felt immediately guilty for rejoicing in someone else's misfortune. *Besides,* she reminded herself severely, *we are forced to believe Thomas is one of them.* Another thought stabbed her. *If he was one of us, there is no surety his heart belongs to me as mine already does to him. Did he not once banish me from Magnus?*

So she set her face into expressionless stone, and stepped forward. He would not get the satisfaction of seeing any delight in her manner.

At her movement into the light, Isabelle shouted. "Flee! He has set a trap!"

In the same moment, Thomas stood abruptly and slashed sideways with his sword.

Both actions froze Katherine, and a thought flashed through her mind. *A warning from Isabelle. They had expected an intruder!*

Katherine was given no opportunity to ponder. A slap of sound exploded in her ears, and a giant hand plucked her feet and yanked her upward. Within a heartbeat, Katherine was helpless, upside down, and flailing her hands at air.

She bobbed once, then twice, then came to a rest, her head at least five feet from the ground.

She swung upside down gently, and Thomas came forward to examine her.

Wonder and shock crossed his face.

"You!" he said.

"This intruder is an acquaintance?" Isabelle asked, her voice laced with scorn.

Thomas turned, and replied patiently, as if instructing a small child. "Your voice is like a screeching of saw blades. Please grace me with silence, unless you choose to answer my questions."

He turned back to Katherine. His face now showed composure.

"Greetings, my lady." He bowed once, then gestured above her. "As you can plainly see, an arrival was not entirely unexpected. My traitorous captive, however, hoped to give you warning."

Katherine crossed her arms to retain her dignity. It was not a simple task, given the awkwardness of holding a conversation while blood drained downward to fill her head. "You may release me," she said. "I have no harmful intentions."

"Ho, ho," Thomas said. A smile played at the corners of his mouth. "You just happened by? It was mere coincidence that my saddlebag is nearly empty of flour?"

Thomas tapped his chin in mock thought. "Of course. You found a trail of flour, and hoped to gather enough to bake bread."

"Your jests fall short of humor," Katherine snapped. "Are they instead meant as weapons in your bag of tricks?"

"You approve, then, of the hidden noose attached to a young sapling?" He savored her helplessness. "All one needs do is release the holding rope with a well-placed swing of the sword, and the sapling springs upward."

The expression on his face became less jovial and his voice slightly bitter. "Another weapon from the faraway land of Cathay. Surely you remember our discussion of that matter in better times. Times of friendship."

Katherine regarded Thomas silently and bit her tongue to keep from replying. This oaf knew so little about the risks she had taken and the sacrifices she had made on his behalf. *How could she ever have dreamed of confiding in him? Even if he offered her half a kingdom, she would not tell him the truth.*

"Without speech, now?" Thomas suddenly became serious with anger. "Magnus has fallen, and like magic you appear, dogging my footsteps when I have avoided all the soldiers of York. From you too I demand answers."

"Thomas, Thomas," another voice chided from behind him. "Emotion clouds judgment."

He whirled to face a figure in black, head hidden by the hood of the dark gown.

"And you! The old man at the gallows!" Thomas said hoarsely. He raised his sword. "I shall end this madness now."

The figure said nothing.

"Before, I had questions," Thomas continued, the strain of holding back his rage obvious in his voice. "And you spoke only of a destiny. Then disappeared."

Thomas advanced on the figure and threatened with his sword. "Now speak. Give me answers or lose your head."

Still no reply.

Thomas prodded the figure with his sword. It collapsed into a heap of cloth.

"You have much to learn," the old man said from the nearby darkness. "Had I chosen, you would have died a dozen times already."

Thomas sagged.

Katherine felt the stirrings of pity for what must be going through him. Anger. Confusion. Desperation. An entire gauntlet of emotions. He must feel intensely weary.

"The fact that you still live should be proof enough that we come in peace," the old man's voice drifted upon him. "Cast your sword aside and we will discuss matters that concern us both. Or the crossbow I have trained upon your heart will end any discussion."

Thomas straightened and regained his noble bearing. Then he dropped his sword.

The old man stepped into view. Unarmed.

He shrugged at the expression that crossed Thomas' face. "No crossbow. A bluff, of course. You are free to grasp your sword. But I think your curiosity is my best defense."

Thomas sighed. "Yes." He pointed to the clothes on the ground. "How was it done?"

Katherine coughed for attention. *Men! Her eyeballs might pop from her head at any moment, and they were more concerned with boasting of techniques of trickery.*

"Simple," the old man replied. "It is merely a large puppet, a crude frame of small branches within the clothes, held extended from string at the end of a pole. With the darkness around it to hold the illusion."

Katherine coughed louder.

Thomas ignored her and nodded admiration at the old man. "A shrewd distraction."

The old man shrugged modestly, then stepped close and whispered, "You are not the only one with access to those books."

Thomas froze at the implications. "Impossible!"

"No?" the old man moved to a log near the fire and sat down. "Please, release poor Katherine. And I shall tell you more."

4

Thomas retrieved his sword, stepped out of the low firelight and approached Katherine where she hung.

He brought his sword back quickly, as if to strike her. A half-smile escaped him at her refusal to flinch.

Barbaric scum. To think I once dreamt of holding you. Katherine did not give Thomas the satisfaction of letting him see her thoughts cross her face.

He slashed quickly at the rope holding her feet and she dropped.

It forced from her a yelp of fright.

Yet somehow, he managed to drop his sword and catch her in one swift movement that cost him a grunt of effort.

For a heartbeat, she was there, in his arms, face only inches from his. And for that heartbeat, she understood why dreams of him had haunted her since banishment from Magnus.

She could not, of course, see the calm gray of his eyes in the darkness of night, but the depth of those eyes remained clear in her memory. She could feel the warmth of his breath as he tightened with the effort of holding her aloft.

The face that looked upon her was—even in the shadows—as she had remembered each morning upon waking. High, intelligent forehead and a straight noble nose. Her right arm had draped around his shoulder as she fell, and against the back of her hand brushed his dark hair. Unlike many of the men in Magnus, Thomas kept his hair long. Tied back, it added strength to the impression immediately given through his square shoulders.

And in the heartbeat of stillness between them, she could sense a strength of quiet confidence earned from an entire winter learning and practicing swordplay.

The total impression in that brief moment was much too enjoyable, and the rush of warmth she could not prevent as he held her became an anger. After all, he had joined the Druid cause. She should not feel what she did to be in his arms.

Her response at the anger she felt toward herself—almost before she realized her left arm was in motion—was to slap him hard across the open face.

He blinked, then set her down gently, but did not take his eyes from her face.

"On this occasion," he said softly, referring to the portion of an evening they had once shared on the ramparts of the castle Magnus, "there was no stolen kiss to deserve such rebuke."

Katherine glared at him, shook the cut rope loose from her ankles, then strode over to rejoin the old man.

Side-by-side, they faced Thomas across the tiny fire.

"You promised to tell me more," Thomas said. "And for that, I would be in your debt." He rubbed his face before continuing. "Although it will take much to convince me of good intentions. And your arrival here was not coincidence. Little encourages me to believe you will speak truth."

How can he pretend so well to be innocent? What monstrous deceit!

Just once, Katherine wished she had not been raised to hold her emotions in control. Just once, she wished she could stamp the ground in frustration and scream between gritted teeth.

Katherine was conscious, however, that Isabelle, still hostage and motionless nearby, was watching her closely. Too closely. So Katherine composed herself to stand in relaxed grace.

The old man answered Thomas.

"We do have much to explain," he said. "There was our first meeting at the gallows—"

Thomas interrupted. "Timed to match the eclipse of the sun. I wish, of course, an explanation for that."

The old man nodded. "Then our midnight encounter as you marched northward to defeat the Scots—"

"With your vague promises of a destiny to fulfill. That too you must answer."

"And finally," the old man continued as if Thomas had not spoken, "Katherine's return to Magnus and her instructions from me which resulted in the trial of ordeal which you survived so admirably."

Thomas shook his head slowly.

"You did not survive?" the old man said in jest. "I see a ghost in front of me?"

"Hardly," Thomas answered with no humor. "You spoke the word 'finally.' There is much more I need to hear. How do you know of my books? What do you know of the Priests of the Holy Grail? Why the secret passages which riddle Magnus? How did you find me in York?"

Thomas paused and delivered his next sentence almost fiercely. *"And what is the secret behind Magnus?"*

The old man shrugged. "I can only tell you what I know."

"Of burning water?" Thomas asked.

Neither Katherine nor the old man were able to hide surprise, even in the low light given by the small flickers of flame.

Thomas pressed. "Of Merlin and his followers?"

The old man sprang forward over the fire and grabbed Thomas by the elbow.

"I advise discretion," he whispered in a hoarse voice. "Your hostage is not as deaf as you once believed."

5

How many times have I done this? Katherine wondered as she stirred her gruel over the open fire. The small pot before her was dented from dozens of similar mornings over dozens of similar fires during her previous travels with the old man.

Only this morning was different.

Across the fire—instead of the old man resting in thoughtful contemplation of the day—sat the captured daughter of a powerful earl who stared at her with open hostility.

Katherine smiled to herself. At least she was not the only one who received those angry stares. Thomas too was marked for hatred by Isabelle's sullen rage.

Not for the first time since rising with the sun's light did Katherine glance at Thomas as he rested against a tree. *Even in the lowly clothes of a monk's assistant, he still appears as noble as the lord of Magnus he once was.*

She quickly turned her head back to the fire. *Stupid child,* she told herself, *appearances are deadly illusions.*

She absently tried to lift the pot away, then sucked in a breath

of pain as the hot metal punished her for her lack of concentration.

*How much did Thomas now know? If only the old man had not
insisted on speaking with Thomas privately last night. If only Isabelle
had not been nearby so that they had been forced to walk far from camp
and leave her behind as guard over the earl's daughter.*

Katherine consoled herself with the thought that it would all
be explained later, when Thomas was fully in their control. For
as the old man had promised, a surprise for that cold-hearted
deceiver truly did wait ahead.

"The girl is expensive baggage," the old man said as Thomas
began to roll up the blankets of camp and pack his saddlebags.

"I agree," Thomas snorted, knowing full well the old man had
meant Isabelle. "However, it was your decision to travel with
Katherine. And mine to depart from you both."

He looked sideways and grinned to see if his jest had struck
the mark. Katherine said nothing, but could not hide the tiny
flushed circles of anger on her cheeks.

Isabelle laughed, but a dark look from Thomas cut her short.

"Merely as a hostage," Thomas said, answering the old man's
original question, "the earl's daughter is worth a fortune. To me,
however, she is even more valuable. Little as the chance is, her
captivity is my only hope to reclaim Magnus."

"Oh?" the old man queried politely.

It was a deceptive tone, for Katherine had discovered often
his mild words were only a prelude to slashing observations
which would destroy the most carefully laid argument.

"Soon she will tire of her silence."

"Oh?"

"Her father rules York only by permission of the Priests of the

Holy Grail, so I am not fool enough to believe that the possibility of her death will frighten the Priests into relinquishing power. But she has knowledge of those priests, and knowledge of the secret circle of Druids. Not until Isabelle tells me all, can I seek to find their weakness, or a way to begin to fight."

"Alone?"

"Despite what you said last night, I cannot place my trust in anyone."

The old man shrugged. "You still need help."

"After Isabelle speaks, she will then be ransomed for gold. That, along with what I have now, will fund a small army. And, as you know, I am not without hidden sources of strategy."

"She is still expensive baggage," the old man commented. "Whatever knowledge she gives you is useless. Whatever army you build is useless. And whatever means of fighting you devise is useless."

Thomas tied down the last saddlebag. "For what you told me last night, I am grateful, if indeed it was truth. As for your advice this morning, I thank you too but, in deference to your age, I must respectfully disagree."

He pulled Isabelle roughly to her feet and tied a rope from her bound wrists to the saddle.

"I am to walk?" she asked in disbelief.

"There are times when chivalry must be overruled by common sense," Thomas said. "You once planned to kill me. I hardly intend to let you control the saddle while I walk."

Thomas swung upward into his saddle. They were ready to depart. Thomas looked at the old man and studiously ignored Katherine.

"Thomas," the old man said. "No amount of force will defeat the Priests of the Holy Grail. Not now. As kings receive their power because all people believe they have a divine right to rule, so now do these priests begin to conquer the land. By the will of the people they deceive."

Thomas froze, only briefly, but enough to show he had suddenly comprehended.

"Yes," the old man continued. "Is it not obvious? Think of how Magnus fell. By consent of the people inside. None dare argue with signs which seem to come from God, no matter how false you and I know those signs to be. First York, then Magnus. Word has reached me that four other towns have been infiltrated, then conquered by these Priests. Soon all of this part of England will belong to them. How long before the entire land is in their control?"

The old man paused.

What had they discussed last night? Katherine wondered. *This sounded like a plea for Thomas to return to them, to join with them and learn the truth behind Magnus, to help in a final battle against the Druids.*

Katherine did not discover the answer.

For the cry of a loud trumpet shrilled through the forest and within moments, the trees around them were filled with the movement of dozens of men, on foot and on horseback, crashing toward them with upraised swords.

She relaxed.

The surprise has arrived as arranged, she thought in triumph. *Thomas will now be our pawn, regardless of his answer.*

Then she cried with horror.

The attackers plunging toward camp wore the battle colors of York. These were knights of the Priests of the Holy Grail.

6

Two lead horses galloped through the camp, scattering the ashes of the fire in all directions. Each rider reined hard and pulled up abruptly beside Thomas and Isabelle.

Within moments, the rest of the camp seemed flooded with men. Some in full armor. Some merely armed with protective vests and swords.

Katherine felt rough hands yank her shoulders. She knew there was little use in struggle, and quietly accepted defeat. A man on each side of her held her arms.

Her attention had been on Thomas.

Now she squirmed slightly to look around her for the old man.

The slight movement earned her an immediate prod in the ribs.

"Pretty or not, m'lady, you'll get no mercy from this sword," came the warning voice in her ear.

Katherine stared straight ahead and endured the arrogant smile that curved across Isabelle's face. Isabelle opened her mouth to speak, but the knight interrupted.

"Greetings from your father," the first knight said to Isabelle. "He will delight to see you safely."

"And you, I am sure, will delight in the reward," she said scornfully as her attention turned to the warrior on his horse.

The knight shrugged.

"Shall my hands remain tied forever?" Isabelle asked.

The knight nodded to one of the men on foot, who stepped forward and carefully cut through her bonds.

Thomas, still in his saddle, had not yet spoken nor moved. His eyes remained focused on Katherine.

Rage and venom. She could feel both from Thomas as surely as if he had spoken those two words.

Yet it was she who should be filled with venom and rage. He had lured them here and sprung this trap to capture them. But the shock of the sudden action had numbed her and she was still far from the first anger of betrayal. A part of her mind wondered about the old man somewhere behind her, surely just as pinned and helpless as she.

Their capture might end what hopes there had been to defeat the Druids. *Would the old man see this as a total defeat? Was he, like her, just beginning to realize the horror that waited ahead?* For neither would reveal their secrets willingly. And both knew well the cruelty of torture which delighted the Druids. Katherine prayed she would die quickly and without showing fear.

"We have them all," the second knight grunted to the first knight beside him. "The girl and her old companion."

He then spoke past Katherine's shoulder. "Someone see that the old man reaches his feet. We have no time to waste."

Reaches his feet?

This time Katherine ignored the point of the sword in her ribs and turned enough to see a heap of black clothing where the old man lay crumpled and motionless.

"Sire, he does not breathe!" protested a nearby foot soldier.

"Who struck him down!" the second knight roared. "Our instructions were—"

The first knight held up a hand to silence him.

"It was I," the first knight said quietly. "The old man leapt in my path, and my horse had no time to avoid him. I believe a hoof struck his head."

No! Katherine wanted to scream. *Impossible!*

For until that moment, she still had held no fear. The old man had been her hope. He would devise a means of escape, even from the most secure dungeon. *He cannot be dead. For if he was, so was she.*

The second knight dismounted, walked past Katherine and knelt beside the old man. He leaned over and checked closely for signs of life.

"Nothing," the knight said in disgust. "We shall be fortunate if our own heads do not roll for this."

He straightened, then glared at the men holding Katherine. "Bind her securely," he said. "But harm not a single hair. Her life is worth not only yours, but every member of your family."

Katherine could not see beyond the blur of her sudden tears. Rough rope bit the skin of her wrists, but she did not feel the pain. Within moments, she had been thrown across the back of a horse, but she was not conscious of inflicted bruises.

The old man was dead. And Thomas was to blame.

7

"**Sit her up properly,**" barked a voice that barely penetrated Katherine's haze of anguish. "She'll only slow our horses if you leave her across the saddle like a sack of potatoes."

Fumbling hands lifted and propped her in a sitting position and guided Katherine's hands to the edge of the saddle. She was too far in her grief to care, too far to fight.

Her mind and heart were so heavy with sorrow that when her tear-blinded eyes suddenly lost all vision, it took her a moment to realize that someone had thrown a hood over her head.

Totally blind, she now had no chance to escape on the horse they had provided her.

Then came a sharp whistle, and her horse moved forward. Slowly, it followed the lead horses in single file down the narrow trail which led back to the main road.

Each step took her farther away from the final sight she would carry always in her mind, that of the old man silent and unmoving among the ruins of camp.

Eventually, the tempo quickened and the steady plodding of her horse became a canter. Katherine had to hold the front edge of the saddle tight with her bound hands and sway in rhythm to keep her balance.

She could hear her own breathing rasp inside the hood as she struggled to keep her balance in the total darkness that blinded her.

By the drumming of hooves she knew other horses were now beside her—instead of front and back—and from that sound she knew the trail had widened. Soon they would be at the main road which led into York.

How far then?

She and the old man—she felt sharp pain twist her stomach to think of him—had walked several hours along the main road yesterday. *That meant less than an hour, if that, on horseback to York. There . . .* she shut her mind. To think of what might lie ahead was to be tortured twice—now and when it actually occurred. And once would be too much.

Would she have a chance to make Thomas pay for his treachery? Even if it was only an unguarded second to lunge at him and rake her nails down his face? Or a chance to claw his eyes?

The cantering of the horses picked up pace.

Her own anger and venom started to burn.

Thomas had arranged this. He had trapped them and led the old man to death. If only there might be a moment to grab a sword and plunge it—

Without warning, the lead horse screamed.

Even as the first horse's scream died, there were yells of fear and the thud of falling bodies and then the screams of men.

Because of the hood over her head, Katherine's world became

a jumble of dark confusion as her own horse stumbled slightly, then reared with panic. The sudden and unexpected motion threw Katherine to the ground at the side of the horse.

A roar of pounding hooves filled her ears and she felt something brush the side of her head.

The horses behind her! Would she be trampled?

Dust choked her gasp of alarm. More thunder of hooves, then a terrible crack of agony that seemed to explode her head into fragments of searing fire.

Then nothingness.

8

The light tickle of a butterfly woke Katherine as it settled on her nose. By the time she realized the identity of the intruder, it had already folded its wings shut.

Despite the deep throb in her head, Katherine suppressed a giggle. Her eyes watered from the effort of crossing them to focus on the butterfly, and even then, the butterfly was little more than a blur of color a scant inch away.

In any other situation, she thought, *this would be a delight. Such a gentle creature honors me with its visit.*

Her memory of the immediate past events returned slowly as the terrible throbbing lessened.

The old man, dead. The procession of horses back to York. Then a terrible confusion. Her fall. Unconsciousness. And now—

And now she could see. The hood no longer covered vision.

Katherine turned her head. Slowly. Not because of the resting butterfly on her nose. But because dizziness filled her stomach at the slight movement.

She discovered she was sitting. Rough bark pressed against

her back. Her hands ... her hands were free.

She brought them up, almost in amazement at the lack of pain biting tightly into her wrists. That movement was enough to startle the butterfly into graceful flight.

"The woman child wakes," a voice said. "And with such prettiness, it is no surprise that even the butterflies seek her attention."

Katherine tensed. The voice belonged to a stranger behind her. Before she could draw her legs in to prepare to stand, he was in front of her, offering a hand to help her rise.

"M'lady," he said. "If you please."

If the man meant harm, he would have done so by now, she told herself. *But what had occurred to bring her here in such confusion?*

When she stood—aware of the rough calluses on the man's hand—she saw the aftermath of that confusion, beyond his shoulders, on the trail between the trees.

Two horses, unnaturally still, lay on their sides in the dust. Several others were tethered to the trunks of nearby trees. She counted four men, huddled at the edge of the trail. Their groans reached her clearly.

"It's an old trick," the man said apologetically, snapping her attention back to him. "We yanked a rope tight across the bend—knee-high to their horses. These fools were traveling in such a tight bunch that when the leaders fell, so did all the others, including you. I offer my apologies for the bandage across your head, but it was a risk we had to take. And we did not know you would be hooded."

Katherine gingerly touched her skull, and found, indeed, a strip of cloth bound just above her ears.

"Your wound was not serious," the man said quickly. "The bandage is merely a precaution."

"Of course," Katherine murmured.

The man shrugged and grinned at her study of his features.

His eyes glinted good humor from beneath shaggy dark eyebrows. His nose was twisted slightly, as if it had been broken at least once, but it did not detract from a swarthy handsomeness, even with a puckered "X"-like scar on his right cheek. His smile, even and white, was proof he was still young, or had once been noble enough to enjoy a diet and personal hygiene which— unlike the diet and hygiene of the less fortunate—did not rot teeth before the owner had reached thirty years of age.

Indeed, traces of nobility still showed in his clothes. The ragged purple cape had once been exquisite, and his balance and posture revealed a confidence instilled by money and good breeding. His shoulders, however, were broad with muscles born of hard work, and the calluses on his hands had not come from a life of leisure. Altogether, an interesting man.

He interrupted her inspection.

"I presume your friend, the old man, escaped?"

His smile faltered as a spasm of grief crossed Katherine's face.

"That," he said gently, "is answer enough."

Katherine nodded. She was spared the embarrassment of showing a stranger unconcealed tears because of someone calling from behind them.

"Robert," a man cried, "come hither."

He beckoned her to follow, and turned to move to the voice. Together, they moved deeper into the trees and moments later entered a small clearing.

Katherine blinked in surprise. The remainder of the enemy horses were gathered. Isabelle sat on one, the two enemy knights on others, Thomas, on the fourth. Each was securely bound with ropes around their wrists. A dozen other men—not of the enemy group—stood in casual circles of two or three among the horses.

"Robert, it is high time we disappeared in the forest," the same voice said.

Katherine identified its owner as an extremely fat and half-bald man in a brown priest's robe.

"Yes, indeed," Robert replied. "The lady seems fit enough to travel." He paused. "Those by the road, they have the ransom note?"

The fat man nodded. "Soon enough they will find the energy to mount the horses we have left for them."

"They're lucky to be alive," spat another man. "I still say we should not bother with this nonsense about the earl's gold."

Robert laughed lightly. "Will, the rich serve us much better when alive." Robert motioned at Isabelle who sat rigidly in her saddle. "The daughter alone is worth three year's wages."

Robert turned to Katherine.

"Yes," he said in a low voice. "We did promise to help the old man by capturing Thomas. But we made no promise about neglecting profit, did we? And although the arrival of these men of York have complicated matters, there is now that much more to be gained by selling these hostages for ransom."

He lifted his eyebrows in a quizzical arch. "After all, as branded kings' outlaws, we can't be expected to be sinless."

9

Their southward march took them so deep into the forest that Katherine wondered how she might find her way back to any road.

The man she knew as Robert led the large but silent procession of outlaws and captives on paths almost invisible among the shadows cast by the towering trees.

It was a quiet journey, indeed almost peaceful. Sunlight filtered through the branches high above them and warmed their backs. The cheerful song of birds seemed to urge them onward.

Twice they crossed narrow rivers, neither deep enough to reach Katherine's feet as she sat securely on the horse Robert had provided. The men on foot had merely grinned and splashed through the water behind her. Katherine hoped each time that Thomas would topple from his own horse and flounder in the water with his hands bound as they were.

Never will that traitor be forgiven.

Again and again as they traveled, she reviewed the morning's horror. *How had Thomas accomplished it? By prearranging his campsite so that the enemy knights knew exactly where to appear?*

Again and again, she fired molten glances of hatred at Thomas' back. *Of course Thomas had known the saddlebag had been leaking flour. To be followed so easily had made his task of flushing them out that much easier. How he must have chuckled as he waited for them in his camp.*

Katherine needed to maintain the hatred. And worse, she realized it herself. Without the hatred to fill her, she would have to face the numbness of the loss of the old man. Without the hatred to consume her, she would have to focus on the struggle ahead. Yet even with the hatred to distract her, questions still managed to trouble her.

With Thomas captured, what was she to do next? Without the old man to guide her, what hopes had she of carrying on the battle against the Druids?

Each time those questions broke through her barrier of hatred, she moaned softly in pain, and forced herself to stare hatred at Thomas' back.

It was after such a moan that the outlaw Robert halted the lead horse. He dismounted, then walked past all the others to reach Katherine.

"M'lady," he began. "We will leave all the horses here and move ahead on foot."

He answered the question without waiting for her to ask it. "A precaution. We near our final destination. The mark of horses' hooves is too easy to follow." Robert gestured at the outlaw named Will. "He will lead the horses to safer grounds."

Katherine nodded, then accepted the hand that Robert offered to help her down from her horse.

"My apologies again," Robert said. "For you, as with the others, must be blindfolded during the final part of our journey."

His grin eased her alarm. "Another precaution. When the king's outlaws hide within the king's forests, it is only natural that we hesitate to show hostages—or visitors—the paths to our camp."

Although none of the outlaws hesitated to call to each other across the camp, their voices were muted with caution.

It could have been the hush of the forest, however. The great trees in all directions blocked whatever wind there might be; the air in their shade was a blanket of stillness.

As the shadows deepened with approaching dusk, small campfires appeared in all directions. At some, there was low singing of ballads. At others, the games of men at rest—arm wrestling, joke telling, and quiet laughter.

The fire at the center of the camp was much larger than any other. Beside it, turning the spit which held an entire deer over the flames, was the fat and half-bald man in a priest's robe. His face gleamed with sweat in the dancing firelight. In his free hand he held a jug of malted water which he replenished often from the cask beside him. A steady parade of men approached with jugs of their own for the same purpose.

Katherine leaned against the trunk of a tree, and watched the proceedings with fascination.

How had the old man known of these outlaws? How had he contacted them? And why had they agreed so readily to help?

At the thought of the old man, her tears—now always so near—began to trickle again.

She blinked them away, then jumped slightly. The outlaw Robert had appeared in front of her in complete silence. *Surely in this darkness*, she thought, *he cannot see my grief.*

"I would bid you join us in our eventide meal," he said. "I am told our venison will be ready soon."

"Certainly," Katherine replied in a steady voice. She did not feel any hunger.

"There is a message I have been requested to relay to you first, however," Robert told her.

Katherine waited.

"Thomas seeks a private audience with you."

The outlaw noticed her posture become stiff.

"Do not fear, m'lady. He is securely bound. A guard is posted nearby."

Katherine noted with satisfaction that her tears had stopped immediately at the prospect of venting her hatred upon Thomas. "Please," she said. "Lead me to him."

The outlaw took her to a small fire set a hundred yards away. As promised, a well-armed guard stood discreetly nearby.

"He is now yours," Robert said. Before departing, he added loudly enough to make sure Thomas received the message. "And m'lady, don't hesitate to call if he disturbs your peace. A sound whipping shall teach him manners."

Katherine nodded and the outlaw Robert slipped away with the same silent steps he had used to approach her.

She then turned to Thomas.

He sat on a log, hands bound in front, a chain around his waist, and attached to the log. Nothing about his posture indicated captivity, however. His nose and chin were held high in pride.

"You requested my presence," Katherine stated coldly.

"Yes, m'lady," Thomas said in a mocking voice. "If it doesn't inconvenience you too much."

Katherine shrugged.

Thomas raised his bound hands and pointed at her and his voice lost all pretense of anything but icy anger.

"I simply want to make you a sworn promise," he said in quiet rage.

"You seem in a poor position to make any promise," she answered with equally calm hatred.

"That will change," Thomas vowed. "And then I will seek revenge."

"Revenge?" she echoed.

"Revenge. To think that I almost believed you and the old man might be friends instead of Druids." He half stood and the chain around his waist stopped him short. "The old man has already paid for his lies with death. And you too will someday regret the manner in which you betrayed my trust."

10

For a moment, Katherine could not get air from her lungs. She opened her mouth once, then twice, in efforts to speak. The shock of his audacity had robbed her of words.

"You ... you ... " she barely managed to sputter.

She looked about wildly and then saw in the nearby underbrush a heavy stick. Rage pushed her onward. She stooped to the stick, pulled it clear, and raised it above her head.

She advanced on Thomas.

He did not move.

"Barbaric fiend!" she hissed. "His life was worth ten of yours!"

She slammed the short pole downward. Thomas shifted sideways in a violent effort to escape and the wood crashed into the log, missing him by scant inches.

It felt too good, the release of her pent-up anger.

She slammed the stick downward again. And again. Each blow slammed the log beside Thomas. He was no longer her target as she mindlessly directed her rage into the sensation of total release. Again and again she pounded downward.

A strange sound reached her through her exhaustion. She realized it was her own hoarse breathing and half-strangled cries of despair between gasps. She realized the heavy pole was now little more than a slivered pulp in her hands. And she realized Thomas stared at her in a mixture of fear and awe.

She poked the splintered pole at his face, and stopped it just short of his eyes.

"You craven animal—" she began, then whirled as the guard's strong hand gripped her shoulder while he spoke in concern. "M'lady—"

"This is none of your concern!" Her rage still boiled, and the guard stepped away in surprise.

She turned back to Thomas and jabbed the wood toward his face again. "How dare you slur his name! He was the finest Merlin of this generation! He was the last hope against you and the rest of the evil you carry! He was—"

Katherine had to stop to draw air. She wavered in sudden dizziness. Then as the last of her rage drained with her loss of energy, she began to cry soundlessly.

She had nothing left inside her but the grief of the old man gone. After forcing back her sorrow for an entire day, she finally mourned the old man's death. The tears coursed down her cheeks and landed softly at her feet.

Blindly, she turned away from Thomas.

His voice called to her. It contained doubt.

"A Merlin?" he asked. "You still insist on posing as a friend?"

"As *your* friend? Never." She could barely raise her voice above a whisper, yet her bitterness escaped clearly. "What you have betrayed by joining them is a battle beyond your comprehension. Yet you Druids shall never find what you seek. Not through me."

"*You* Druids!" His voice began to rise again with rage. "I am exiled from Magnus. A bounty on my head! And you accuse *me* of belonging to those sorcerers?"

Katherine drew a lung full of breath to steady herself. "You knew we watched," she said. "Your masters sent you forth from York with the Earl's daughter as bait for us."

"Sent me forth? Your brains have been addled by the fall. I risked my very life to take her hostage."

Katherine managed a snort. "Pray tell," she said with sarcasm. "How convenient, was it not, that the drawbridge remained open for you, and not the pursuing knights? And explain how you managed to reach the earl inside the castle, even though he had been forewarned."

Thomas gaped. "Forewarned? You speak in circles."

Another snort. "Hardly. You pretend ignorance."

They stared at each other.

Finally Thomas leaned forward and asked in a low voice, "Who, then forewarned the earl, if not you, the people who managed to follow me when none other knew my plans?"

Had it been less dark, Thomas would have seen clearly the contempt blazing from Katherine's eyes. "I was a fool for you," she said. "Caring for you in the dungeon of Magnus when even then your master Waleran was there. Then to discover him nearby in York . . . "

Thomas now gasped. "Waleran? In York? How did you know?" He stiffened in sudden anger. "Unless," he accused, "you are one of them. Leading those knights to my camp."

More moments of suspicious silence hung between them.

"Why?" Katherine then asked softly. "Why do you still pretend? And why did you betray us so badly? Is it not enough you were given the key to the secret of Magnus at birth?"

Thomas spoke very softly. "I pretend nothing. I betray no one. And this secret of Magnus haunts me worse than you will ever know."

He continued in the same gentle, almost bewildered tones.

"Katherine, if we fight the same battle, whoever betrayed us both would take much joy to see us divided."

Thomas shook his head. "And if you are one of them, may God have mercy on your soul for this terrible game of deceit you play."

"M'lady, what plans have you for the morrow?" Robert asked. Now, with dawn well upon them, lazy smoke curled upward from the dying fires.

Katherine huddled within her cloak against the chill of early day. She stood, where she had remained motionless for the last four hours, staring at the embers of the campfire nearest her.

"M'lady?"

With visible effort, Katherine pulled herself from her thoughts, and directed her gaze at the outlaw Robert.

"Plans? I cannot see beyond today."

It was said with such despair that Robert gently took her elbow and guided her—for she did not resist—to the main campfire where the fat outlaw now stirred a wooden paddle in a large iron pot.

"Broth," Robert directed the fat man. "She needs broth."

With catlike grace that showed surprising nimbleness for such a large man, a bowl was brought forth and filled to the brim from the pot.

Robert helped Katherine lift the bowl to her mouth. When she tried to set it down after a tiny sip, he forced it back to her mouth again. And again. Until finally, enough warm salty soup had trickled down her throat to make her realize that she was famished.

Greedily, she gulped the soup, then held it out for more.

The outlaw Robert smiled in satisfaction. He waited until she had finished two more bowls, then led her to a quiet clearing away from camp.

"Tell me," he said, "what plans have you for the morrow?"

Katherine stood straighter now, and much of the wild hopelessness had disappeared from her eyes.

"None." She smiled wanly. "Not yet."

"I have discovered," Robert said slowly, "that to make plans one must first decide one's goal. Then it is merely a matter of finding the easiest path to that goal."

Despite herself, Katherine chuckled. "Knowing the goal, my friend, presents little difficulty. The path to that goal?" She shrugged. "One might as well plan a path across open sky."

The outlaw shrugged. "The task is not that impossible. After all, birds fly."

"They are not armed with weapons to destroy."

"M'lady, what is it you want?"

Katherine thought of the secrets she had shared so long with the old man. Sadly, she said, "I cannot say."

The outlaw studied her face, then said quietly, "So be it. But if I, or my men can be of service ... "

Katherine, in return, studied the older man's face, almost as if seeing it for the first time. "Why is it," she asked, "that you offer so much? First to rescue me and capture Thomas. And now this?"

"The old man never told you?"

Katherine shook her head.

"We had been captured once," the outlaw said. He rubbed the x-like scar on his cheek. "Captured and branded like slaves. Held in the dungeons of York. The rats and fleas our only companions. The night before our execution, all the guards fell asleep ... "

Robert's face reflected wonderment. "Each guard, asleep like a baby, and suddenly the old man appeared among them. One by one, he unlocked our doors and set us free."

Katherine hid her smile. *Child's play for one of the Merlins. A tasteless sleeping potion in food or wine. But why the rescue of these particular outlaws? What had the old man intended?*

"When?" Katherine asked. "When did this happen?"

"Some years ago," the outlaw replied. "We learned our lesson well. Since then, the sheriff's men have not seen so much as a hint of us."

He grinned. "Except, of course, through the complaints of those we rob."

He went on quickly at Katherine's frown. "Only those corrupted by power," Robert explained. "Those who will never face justice because they control the laws of the land."

"You will continue to be a thorn in the sides of those who reign now, the Priests of the Holy Grail?"

"It will be our delight to provide such service."

A new thought began to grow in Katherine's mind. She spoke aloud. "My duty," she said, "is to fight them also. No matter how hopeless my cause might seem, I must strive against them."

Robert nodded. He understood well the nobility of effort.

"I have little chance to succeed," Katherine continued. "But what chance there is, I must grasp with both hands."

"Yes?" Robert sensed she had a request.

"Offer to battle Thomas. Set the stakes high. His life to be forfeited if he loses or his freedom if he wins."

"M'lady?"

Katherine spoke strongly, more sure each passing second of what she must do in the next weeks. "Then," she said, "make certain that you lose the battle."

"As you wish, m'lady." The outlaw bowed. "Or my name is not Robert Hood."

THOMAS
Exile Begins
LATE SPRING A. D. 1313

"**I've already said it once.** Board this vessel alone, or not at all."

Thomas, in reply, merely shifted the puppy beneath his arm to the other. It was a deliberate act, done slowly to show he had no fear of the loud sailor. It was also a difficult act. The cloak Thomas wore did not encourage his movement. Yet he would not ever consider traveling without the cloak—Thomas understood well why the old man who had deceived him wore such a garment. It concealed much of what he must always carry hidden upon him.

The sailor facing him jabbed a dirty finger in the air to make his point. "You, a dog, and all its fleas. Hah! Might you be thinking this is Noah's ark?"

The sailors around him—always eager to watch a confrontation—laughed loudly.

"Aargh! Noah's ark!" The laughter continued in waves as that joke was passed from crewman to crewman.

Silence finally settled upon them, broken only by the constant screaming of gulls as they dipped and swooped for the choicest pieces of garbage on the swells of the gray water beside them.

"This puppy once saved my life," Thomas said quietly. "You will receive full passage for the creature."

The sailor squinted. "Eh? You'll pay double just to keep the mongrel beside you across the North Sea?"

Thomas nodded.

They stood on the edge of a great stone pier that jutted into the Scarborough harbor. Because of his history lessons in the abbey from a childhood nurse long since dead, Thomas knew how ancient this harbor town was.

More than 1,200 years earlier, Roman soldiers had built a signal post behind a rough wooden palisade on the edge of the cliffs that rose high and steep directly north of the harbor. From there, they could see approaching war ships and send messages forty miles inland to York for legions of soldier reinforcements.

In later centuries, Scarborough had suffered—as had most of the coastal towns—under the lightning quick raids of the bloodthirsty Vikings. Time and again the Norsemen had sailed into this same harbor and forced the townspeople to scurry up the paths that led to the castle walls which now lined the edge of the cliff above them. Time and again they had watched helplessly while those Vikings looted the houses which clustered the harbor, and killed and tortured those too slow to reach the castle in time.

Those Vikings had found the English land so rich that it ultimately defeated them with promises of luxury—eventually they began to settle it and intermarry. Then, in the year 1066, those Anglo-Saxons suffered defeat by the French through their Norman invasions. Through it all, Scarborough had served well as a harbor town, nearly as important as the major coastal city of Hull, a few days travel to the south.

Now, as Thomas' nostrils informed him, Scarborough thrived and bustled with the activities of fishing and merchant boats.

Around him: the stench of rotten fish, of their entrails discarded carelessly in the water, of salt-crusted damp wood forever soaked with fish blood, and of mildewed nets.

He prayed thanks again for finding the *Dragon's Eye*, a merchant ship, one which was already near full with bales of wool from the sheep grown on the hills of the inland moors. He prayed thanks again for finding one of the few merchant ships not owned by the Flemings or Italians. Now at least, he could barter his passage in English.

After that brief moment of prayer, he looked directly into the sailor's eyes, bloodshot and bleary above a matted beard.

"Double passage," Thomas repeated firmly. To prove his point, he dug into his small purse for another piece of gold.

The act of keeping the puppy beneath an arm while using the same hand to hold the purse proved tricky however, and as the puppy squirmed slightly, it knocked the purse loose.

A dozen gold coins spilled across the stone.

Thomas knelt quickly and scooped them into his free hand. But it was much too late. When he stood, he faced the heat of greedy stares from all directions.

The sailor in front of him coughed politely.

"We welcome you aboard. And your companion." The sailor smiled, but there was no kindness in his eyes. "It would appear you both deserve to be treated like kings."

13

A deckhand led Thomas to the rear of the *Dragon's Eye*, and chattered like a man who was far too accustomed to lonely weeks at sea with a crew of only eighteen, none with anything new to discuss.

"You picked a fine ship, you did," the deckhand said. "A cog like this handles the roughest seas."

The cog was over a 100 feet long, with a deep and wide hull to hold the bulkiest of cargos. Thomas stepped around the bales of wool. Above him, the single sail was furled around the thick, high center mast. Thomas had seen cogs leaving the harbor with open sails, and knew the square sail was large enough to drive the boat steadily in front of any wind.

"It's not fast, nor an easy boat to maneuver," the deckhand continued in the voice of one happy to have the chance to finally impart knowledge to someone who knew less than he, "but it's almost impossible to capsize."

He lowered his voice. "And its high sides make it difficult to be boarded at sea by pirates."

He smiled at the result he had hoped to achieve. Thomas' face had darkened with sudden concern.

"Look about you," the deckhand waved. "The castle at the prow—" His voice became smug. "*Fighting tower at the front* is how I should explain it proper for you land people, lets us fire arrows and such from above at any raiders who draw close."

He then waved at their destination on the cog, ahead of them by some 50 feet and stack after stack of bundled wool. "The stern castle—tower at the rear—is for important guests."

The deckhand sighed. "A bed and privacy. What gold can't buy!"

Then he remembered he had superiority because of his knowledge and immediately began lecturing again. "We've got oars— we call them sweeps—should the gales be too rough or should we need to outrun pirates. You might be asked to man one then."

Now Thomas said or did nothing to stop the flow of words which he barely heard.

Dangerous gales and pirate attacks. What folly had brought him here? The words of an old man who had betrayed him. And some vague references in his secret books. Such madness to begin the journey, let alone hope in its success.

Yet what else was there to do? The reward on his head had been increased, and with the Priests of the Holy Grail slowly controlling town after town, there soon would be no place safe left for him in northern England. Unless he chose to live the uncertain life of an outlaw, and his contest for life and freedom against that wily Robert Hood had shown how dangerous that might be—

The deckhand interrupted his thoughts. "Here you are. The stern castle. My advice is that you tie the dog inside. There'll be enough grumbles about a dog enjoying the shelter denied us crew without his presence outside as a daily reminder."

Thomas nodded.

The deckhand hesitated, an indication he knew he should not ask. But his curiosity was too strong. "Our destination is Lisbon. Do you intend to go beyond Portugal?"

The scowl he received from Thomas was answer enough.

You and your friends stared at my scattered coins like wolves at a lamb, Thomas thought. *And I'm fortunate we depart before you hear about the gold offered for my head. The less you know the better.*

The deckhand stumbled back awkwardly to make room for Thomas to enter the dank and dark stern castle.

Thomas finished his thoughts as he ducked inside. *And most certainly the Druid spies will someday discover I escaped England on the* Dragon's Eye, *and eager will be the sailors to impart that information for the slightest amount of gold. They cannot know my destination is that of the Last Crusaders. Jerusalem. The Holy City.*

1 4

If the deckhand believes this to be luxury, Thomas thought with a sour grin, *then he and all the crew have my sympathy.*

As if in agreement at the squalor of the dark and cramped quarters—hardly more than walls and a low roof—the puppy beneath his arm whined.

"You like it neither?"

Thomas set the puppy down on the rough wood floor. It shivered, then crawled beneath a crude bed.

"They told us two weeks to Lisbon if the weather is favorable," Thomas told his now unseen companion. "And crossed themselves when I asked how long if the weather wasn't."

Another answering whine.

Thomas smiled. A week earlier, the puppy had first growled fearlessly as Thomas entered the cave after the absence of several days, caused, of course, by the time spent captive among Robert Hood and his outlaws. The fearless growls had then changed to yips of total joy as the puppy had recognized Thomas' scent.

Thomas had responded to the barking and jumping with equal joy, something which had surprised him greatly. True, he had not had intentions of leaving the dog to die slowly in the cave—and indeed had worried upon his capture that the puppy would die the slow lingering death of starvation—but Thomas did not want to be burdened with concern for anything except his goal of winning Magnus. And, until that joy at their reunion had so surprised him, he had intended to leave the puppy somewhere with peasants.

Instead, he had decided not to abandon the puppy, then had spent two days in the cave, pouring through the ancient pages of knowledge, or staring in thought at the natural rock chimney which allowed sunlight to enter, uncaring of the aches which still battered his every move because of the fierce fight against the outlaw Robert Hood.

Those two days he had puzzled his next move. Yes, Magnus seemed out of reach. But the quest for Magnus had been instilled almost before he had learned to run, by the childhood nurse who had replaced the parents he had never seen.

Without Magnus to pursue, what else had he in life?

So, despite the near impossibility of his task—an impossibility he knew full well—he could not let it go.

And at the end of the second day of silence in the cave near the abbey where he'd spent his childhood, Thomas had decided the only and slimmest chance of victory would be in uncovering the very reason that the books had been hidden where they were. The only clues he had were vague references to the Last Crusade, written in the page margins of two of the books. And simply because they were too similar to what he had heard from the mysterious old man during their midnight discussion before the betrayal, he had realized he could not ignore what it meant.

A sudden wave nearly pitched him against the far wall of his quarters. He recovered his balance, but realized the wave was a brutal reminder of the obstacles ahead. *Had he chosen right the direction of his search? To be wrong meant a year wasted, one more year for the Priests of the Holy Grail to add strength to their hold over the area around Magnus.*

Thomas knelt—too keenly aware of the swaying of the boat—and did as he had been taught. He poured out his troubles in prayer. That quiet moment brought him peace. After all, in the face of the Almighty—the One who counts years as seconds and who promises love beyond comprehension for eternity—what mattered a man's gravest troubles when that promised eternity made any life on earth—troubled or untroubled—the briefest of flashes?

Strive to do your best here on earth, Thomas could hear a patient voice echo in his mind, *yet in all your pursuit, remember and take heart that it is only the first step toward something much greater.*

At that thought, Thomas' eyes watered. Gentle and kind Gervase, the calm speaker of that lesson, now too, like that long ago childhood nurse, had passed from this life. And in a near-hopeless effort to save Magnus.

God rest their souls, Thomas finished his prayer with a sudden determination to continue his quest, if only because of the sacrifices others had made, *and God be here on these cold gray waters with mine.*

Thomas opened his eyes and prepared himself for the beginning of a voyage which gave him little hope of return to England, let alone any victory to defeat the Druids who held Magnus.

The first fight for his life took place after only three days at sea.

15

By then, shortly after dawn on the third morning, Thomas wanted to die anyway.

"Carry your own bucket out," snarled the sailor into the cramped quarters as Thomas sat weakly hunched over his knees on the edge of his bed. "We've no time for soft-headed fools around here."

The sailor half dropped and half threw the bucket in Thomas' direction, then slammed the door in departure.

Thomas could not even lift his head to protest. A small part of his mind was able to realize that the deckhand's prediction about resentment because of the puppy had been proven right. For two days, food had been brought to his quarters. For two days, each visitor bearing that food—except for a small, dirty cook's assistant who had stooped to let the puppy lick his hands—had grumbled about the waste of good food and valuable space for anything as useless as a mere dog.

The larger part of his mind, however, thought nothing about the puppy or the obvious resentment among the crew.

Thomas truly wanted to die.

The cog—as promised by the first deckhand—rode the rough seas with no more danger of sinking than if it had been a cork. However, like a cork, it tossed and bobbed on top of the long gray swells of water as the winds slowly took the cog south through the English Channel and into the vast North Atlantic Ocean.

Only once had Thomas been able to stagger to the door of his quarters to look out upon those waves, green-gray and hardly any different in color than the bleak sky. The waves had seemed like small mountains, bearing down on the vessel without mercy, lifting it high, then throwing it down again, only to be lifted by the next rushing surge of tons of water.

That sight had propelled him back into the quarters again, where he had fallen to his knees and emptied what little remained of the contents of his stomach.

Thomas was seasick. It did not help that the food offered with such little grace consisted of biscuits and salted herring and malted water. Merely the smell of the food within the bucket was often enough to make Thomas heave again into another and smaller bucket designed to serve as a portable latrine.

His companion, the puppy, seemed oblivious to the sea. Indeed, it seemed to delight in the pitches and rolls of the ship, and bounded around the small quarters with enthusiasm.

"Traitor," Thomas muttered to the puppy as it now attacked the contents of the bucket. "Is it no wonder you grow like a weed, taking my portion with such greed?"

The puppy did not bother to look up.

A vicious wave slammed the side of the cog, and knocked Thomas a foot sideways.

He groaned at the nausea that overwhelmed him, and prepared for the now familiar tightening and release of his stomach and ribs racked with renewed pain as he leaned over the slop bucket and violently threw up.

The cold wind bit the skin of his face and throat and provided Thomas a slight measure of relief as he lurched from his quarters at the rear of the ship.

Below him, in the belly midship, was the crude tent-like roof of cloth that sheltered the crew from the wind and inevitable rain. Men moved in and out of the shelter, all intent on their various duties.

Thomas carried the slop bucket to the side of the ship and braced his legs to empty it over the side. He was so weak that it took all of his energy and concentration to keep his balance and not follow the contents overboard.

He turned back to retrace the few steps to his quarters. And nearly stumbled into the large sailor who blocked his path.

"By the beard of old Neptune himself," the sailor said with a nasty grin, "you would favor us all by becoming food for the fish yourself."

Thomas saw something as cold as the North Atlantic in the man's eyes, and beyond the man's shoulder he saw that two other sailors were entering his quarters. He understood the implications immediately.

"I had feared pirates at sea," Thomas said. He had to swallow twice to find the strength to continue, and was angry at the weakness showed so clearly. "But I did not expect them aboard this vessel."

The sailor leaned forward, yellow eyes above a dirty beard. "Pirates? Hardly. We saw the color of your gold and know the ship's captain charged too little by far for us to bear the insult of living so poorly while a dog lives so well."

Thomas sucked in lungfuls of cold air, hoping to draw from it a clearness that would rid him of his nausea.

"Rate of passage is the captain's realm," he finally said.

The sailor took Thomas' hesitation as fear, and laughed. "Not when the captain sleeps off a night's worth of wine!"

There was a loud yelp from the quarters, then a muffled curse. The other two sailors backed out. One held his hand in pain. The other held the puppy by the scruff of his neck.

"No signs of coin anywhere," the sailor with the puppy said. He dangled the puppy carelessly, and ignored its small whines of pain.

The other sailor grimaced and squeezed his bleeding hand. "That whelp of Satan took a fair chunk from my thumb."

The yellow-eyed sailor turned back to Thomas. He dropped his hand to his belt and with a blur of movement, pulled free a short dagger.

He grinned black teeth.

"Consider your choices lad. 'Tis certain you carry the gold. You'll hand it over now. Or lose a goodly portion of your neck."

1 6

Again, from the sailor's yellow eyes gleamed a coldness which could belong to no sane man. Thomas knew the sailor was lying—once they had the gold, he would die anyway. Alive, he would later be able to complain to the captain, or once ashore, seek a local magistrate. The sure solution for them was to make sure no one was watching this far corner of the ship, and toss him—alive or dead—overboard. Then, no person aboard the ship would be able to prove their crime.

Show weakness, Thomas commanded himself, *your only chance against three is to lull them into expecting no fight at all.*

He sagged, an easy task considering the illness that seemed to bring his stomach to his throat.

"I beg of you," Thomas cried, "spare my life! You shall receive all I have!"

The evil grin of blackened teeth widened.

"Of course we'll spare your life," the yellow-eyed sailor promised. He jabbed his knife forward. "Your coin!"

All three laughed at how quickly Thomas cowered in reaction

to the movement of the knife.

Then Thomas fumbled with his cloak. "I keep it in a pouch hanging from my neck," he said, not needing much effort to place an extra quaver in his voice. "T'will take but a moment."

Long before—it now seemed like a lifetime—Thomas had once shared the dungeon cells of Magnus with Sir William, a knight from a faraway land. The knight had shown him the design of a leather sheath which was strapped around his upper body, so that a sword might remain hidden high on his back, between his shoulder blades. The knight had shown him the art of drawing the sword quickly, a Roman short sword capable of deadly work in close quarters. Later, when both were free from the danger and away from prying eyes, the knight had made Thomas practice the move again and again.

Reach for your neck, as if scratching a flea, the knight had said, *then in one motion, lean forward, draw it loose, and slash outward at your enemy.*

"The knot is awkward," Thomas explained in a stammering voice as he fumbled with his right hand at his throat. He bent forward slightly, as if reaching behind his neck for a knotted string of leather. "But it will only take—"

He did not finish.

The hours of training had not been wasted.

In one silky smooth move, the sword drew free beneath his ducked head. Head still down, he struck at the spot he had memorized before bending—the knife hand of the yellow-eyed sailor.

A solid *thunk* and squeal of pain rewarded him, even as he raised his head to give him a clear view of all three.

The sailor's knife bounced off the wood deck.

Without pause, Thomas kicked fiercely the yellow-eyed sailor, sinking his foot solidly into the man's groin. Then, even as the man fell forward in agony, Thomas charged ahead, slashing sideways and cutting steel into the flesh of the second sailor's shoulder.

The third sailor only managed to step back half a pace, but even in that time had brought his arm back to cast the puppy overboard.

He froze suddenly.

"I think not," Thomas grunted.

The sailor did not disagree. He slowly lowered the puppy, careful not to move in any way that might encourage Thomas to press any harder with the point of the sword pressed into the hollow of his throat.

"Let the puppy fall," Thomas said softly. "He'll find his feet. And you might not find your head."

The sailor could not even nod, so firmly was the sword lodged against his flesh. He simply opened his hand. The puppy landed softly, then growled and bit the sailor's ankle. Tears of pain ran down the man's face, but no sound could leave his throat.

"Obey carefully. This sword may slip," Thomas warned. "My balance on these pitched waves has proven difficult."

The sailor's eyes widened in agreement.

Thomas pointed left with his free hand, and the sailor slowly shuffled in that direction. Thomas kept the sword in place, and shuffled right, and in that manner of a grotesque dance, they continued until Thomas had half circled, and now faced the other two wounded sailors.

The puppy stood directly between his legs and growled upward at all three sailors.

"Listen to him well," Thomas said. All three sailors bled soundlessly. The yellow-eyed one with the bones showing on the back of his hand. The second one with a gash through sleeve and shoulder. And the third from a torn ankle.

"Listen to my friend well," Thomas repeated. "The next time

your greed will cost you your lives."

Even as the next words left his mouth, however, Thomas knew by the hatred from their eyes that they would return. Yet he was helpless, for he would have to betray every instinct he held to kill them now in cold blood.

God help me, he prayed silently, *if they catch me unawares again.*

1 8

Thomas could only guess the time when he next left his quarters, for low and angry gray skies hid the sun's location.

He grinned upward despite the bleakness of the forbidding sky and endless swells of water. Dizziness and nausea had finally left him. After days without food, after days of constant vomiting, he was famished.

He carried the empty food bucket and swayed in rhythm to the motion of the ship as he walked to the edge of the rear deck. From there, he slowly studied the movements of the crew below.

Nothing seemed threatening.

For a moment, he considered seeking the ship's captain to set forth his accusations against the three.

Then he dismissed the idea. Whose side would the captain choose? Certainly not his. With a crew of eighteen men—mostly unhappy with Thomas because of the puppy's comfort—the captain would never risk becoming the focus of all anger by trying to discipline one-sixth of the crew.

No, Thomas could only pray that he had shown enough willingness to fight that the crewmen would not feel it worth the effort to provide more trouble.

Yet, there was the sailor with the yellow eyes.

Thomas felt the man would return. And probably when all advantages were his. It would be a long, long journey, Thomas told himself, even if the cog were to reach Lisbon in the next hour. And there were weeks ahead.

A slow, small movement below demanded his attention and tore him from his thoughts.

Yet, as he had been taught, Thomas refrained from glancing immediately at its source. No, by yawning and stretching and swivelling his head as if he had a sore neck, he was able to direct his gaze at the movement without showing any interest.

Only the cook's assistant. Hat over eyes, shifting in sleep in a corner away from the constant menial work of preparing food.

Thomas looked elsewhere. Only briefly. The weight of the empty bucket was an unnecessary reminder of his intense hunger.

Thomas whistled, low and sharp.

He sleeps soundly.

Thomas whistled again. This time, the cook's assistant raised his head and opened his bleary eyes.

Thomas waved for him to approach the short ladder that led up to his quarters from the main deck of the cog.

"I beg forgiveness for waking you," Thomas began, for he could remember his own days of back-grinding labor and little rest. "But I grow faint with hunger."

Thomas lifted his empty bucket and smiled. "You could earn yourself a friend."

The cook's assistant shrugged, face lost in shadows beneath the edge of the battered leather cap, and took the offered bucket. When he returned, Thomas climbed down the ladder, reached into the bucket and used his teeth to tear apart a hard biscuit. He swallowed water from a jug in great gulps, and then filled his mouth with the salted herring.

Thomas ate frantically in silence, half grinning in apology between bites. When Thomas finally finished, he wiped his mouth clean with the sleeve of his cloak.

"You have my gratitude," Thomas stated with good-natured fervor.

Once again, the cook's assistant shrugged, then held out his hand for the bucket.

"A moment, please," Thomas asked. "Have you any news of three crewmen in foul tempers?"

Raised eyebrows greeted that question. *What face I can see is so dirty,* Thomas thought, *hair so filthy he is fortunate it is cut too short to support so many fleas. And his clothes are hardly more than layers and layers of rags.*

"Of course," Thomas laughed at the silent response to his question. "All sailors have foul tempers."

A guarded smile greeted his joke.

"Three men," Thomas prompted, "with wounds in need of care. Has any gossip regarding their plans reached your ears?"

Another shrug. Then the cook's assistant touched his forefinger to his own lips.

Thomas understood. *Mute.*

The cook's assistant set the bucket down and cupped his hands together, palms upward. He then stroked with one hand the air above the other.

"Puppy?" Thomas asked. "You inquire of its well being?"

The cook's assistant nodded, almost sadly.

"Its belly is fat with the food I could not eat." Thomas smiled lazily, happy to be seasick no longer. "At least only one of us needed to suffer."

The cook's assistant opened his hands wide.

"Why?" Thomas interpreted. "Why so much trouble for a worthless puppy?"

He answered his own question. "That small, worthless creature saved my life."

Then, speaking more to himself than to his audience, Thomas said very softly. "And it is the only living thing I dare trust."

They attacked when the moon was at its highest.

The clouds had broken in early evening, some six hours earlier, and the water had calmed shortly after. The dark of night then provided peace to the weary crew. While the constant creaking of the ship continued, no longer did it groan and strain with every wave.

Thomas saw every move of their advance.

Crouched low, and silent with stealth, they slipped from bale to bale until reaching the ladder.

There were only three.

Thomas smiled. Whatever code sailors had, it probably contained some of the rules of knighthood. Since Thomas had shown bravery by fighting earlier in the day, the other sailors had probably decided he should be left alone.

If the other crew members had refrained from joining the attack, however, they had done nothing to prevent these three from waiting until the stillest hour of the night to finish their crime.

Thomas smiled again.

The sailor at the rear limped each step. *Ah, puppy's teeth left their mark.*

Thomas could enjoy the observation of their deadly approach because he was far from his quarters, hidden in the shadows of bales of wool. Far too easy, should the opportunity arise, for an unwary sleeper to be trapped inside those quarters, and far too easy a knife of revenge drawn across his throat. So he had chosen the discomfort of the open ship.

Seek what treasures you will, Thomas thought merrily. *Seek it until dawn. For what you desire rests safely with me.*

Within his cloak lay his gold. Warm against his side lay the puppy, squirming occasionally with dreams.

I shall rest during the day, Thomas silently promised the three sailors, *and spend my nights at constant guard among these shadows.*

Much to his satisfaction, angry whispers reached Thomas. There was a light bang of the door shutting, and a grunt of pain. More angry whispers.

Then silence. Minutes of silence.

It began to stretch his nerves, knowing they were above him, out of sight, about to appear in silhouette at the top of the ladder at any moment.

Thomas wanted the warning, wanted to know as soon as possible when they were about to descend. But he did not stare at the top of the ladder.

Instead, he chose to focus on a point beyond it. Night vision, he knew, caught movement much more efficiently at the sides of the eyes.

Silence continued. Now the creaking of the ship seemed to be the low haunting cries of spirits.

Suddenly, Thomas' heart leapt in the terror of shock.

Directly above him, the edge of the deck detached itself!

He managed not to flinch, then forced himself to be calm and slowly, very slowly, turned his head to see more clearly.

The black edge of the deck had redefined itself to show the black outlines of a man's head and shoulders.

These men are shrewd. They have decided I must be hidden nearby. Instead of choosing the obvious—the ladder—they now watch from above, hoping I will not notice and betray myself with a movement.

Thomas told himself he was safe as long as he remained still. After all, he had chosen a deep shadow.

Yet, his heart continued to hammer at a frantic pace. *This is what the rabbit fears, hidden among the grass. I understand now, the urge to bolt before the hounds.*

But Thomas did not.

Instead, what betrayed him was the only creature he trusted.

The puppy, deep in dreams, yelped and squirmed.

And within seconds, two of the sailors dropped to the belly of the ship. One from each side of the upper deck.

The puppy yelped again, and they moved with unerring accuracy to the bale which hid him.

Moonlight glinted from extended sabers.

Thomas barely had time to stand and withdraw his own sword before they were upon him.

"**A shout for help will do no good,**" came a snarl with the approach of the first. "The captain's drunk again, and the crew have turned a blind eye."

"For certes," a harsh whisper followed. "None take kindly to the manner in which you crippled my hand."

Thomas said nothing, only waited with his sword in front.

The puppy, now awake, pressed against his leg in fear.

Another movement as the third sailor, the one with the limp, scuttled down the ladder from the upper deck. He too brandished a saber.

I have been well trained, thought Thomas, *by Robert of Uleran, the man who fell in my defense at Magnus. I shall not disappoint his memory by now falling myself without a worthy fight.*

The sailors circled Thomas, shuffling slowly in the luxury of anticipation. The silver light of the moon made it an eerie dance.

Impossible to watch all three at once.

From where will the first blow come?

Thomas heard the whistle of steel slicing air, and instinctively stepped back. He felt a slight pull against the sleeve of his cloak, then—it seemed like an eternity of waiting later—a bright slash of pain and the wetness of blood against his arm.

"Ho, ho," the yellow-eyed sailor laughed. "My weaker hand finds revenge for the damage you did the other!"

The sailors circled more.

One dodged in and dodged back, daring Thomas to attack, daring Thomas to leave the bale behind him and expose his back.

The others laughed in low tones.

This is the game. Cats with a cornered mouse. They are in no hurry.

"Gold and your life," the second sailor whispered. "But only after you beg to be spared."

The other two chortled agreement.

Until that moment, Thomas had felt the deep cold of fear. His blood would soak the rough wood at his feet, that he knew. But their taunts filled him with a building anger and his fear became distant.

"Beg?" Thomas said in a voice he hardly recognized as his. "Shall I die, you will die with me. This is a fight which will cost you dearly."

The yellow-eyed sailor mimicked his voice with a high-pitched giggle. "This is a fight which will cost you dearly."

That slow growing anger suddenly overwhelmed Thomas. He became quiet with a fury that could barely be restrained.

He lifted his sword and pointed it directly at the yellow-eyed sailor and spoke with compressed rage. "You shall be the first to taste doom."

The yellow-eyed sailor slapped his neck. Then, incredibly, as Thomas lowered his sword to a protective stance, the yellow-eyed sailor sank to his knees, then soundlessly fell face forward onto the deck.

What madness is this?

Thomas had no time to wonder. The second sailor betrayed a movement and Thomas whirled to face him. Still carried by that consuming rage, Thomas pointed his sword at the man's eyes.

The man grunted with pain, eyes wide and gleaming with surprise in the moonlight. He too dropped to his knees and tumbled forward to land as heavily as a sack of fish.

What madness is this?

Thomas answered his own bewilderment. *Whatever it might be, this is not the time to question.*

He spun on the third sailor, who now staggered back in fear. Thomas raised his sword and advanced.

"Nooo!" the man shrieked loudly in terror. "Not me!"

Then he gasped, as if slapped hard across the face. His mouth gaped open, then shut before he pitched forward.

That shriek had pierced the night air, and from behind Thomas, came the sounds of men moving through the ship.

He gathered his cloak about him, scooped the puppy into his other arm, and fled toward the ladder.

1 9

Thomas had fourteen nights and fifteen days to contemplate the miracle which had saved his life, fourteen nights and fifteen days of solitude to puzzle the events. For not a single member of the crew dared disturb him.

The three sailors had risen the next day from stupor, unable to explain to the crew members who had dragged them away what evil had befallen them at the command of Thomas' sword.

Each day, the cook's assistant had been sent with food. Each day the cook's assistant had darted away without even the boldness to look Thomas in the eye.

While fourteen nights and fifteen days was enough time for the shallow slice on his arm to heal, it was not enough time for Thomas to make sense of those scant minutes of rage beneath the moonlight.

Many times, indeed, he had taken his sword and pointed it at objects around him, disbelieving that it might have an effect, but half expecting the object to fall or move, so complete was his inability to understand how he in his rage had been able to fell three sailors intent on his death, *without touching one.*

And for fourteen nights and fifteen days, he fought the strange sensation that he *should* know what had happened. That somewhere deep in his memory, there was a vital clue in those strange events.

On the sixteenth day, he remembered. Like a blast of snow-filled air, it struck him with a force that froze him midway through a troubled pace.

No, it cannot be!

Thomas strained to recall words that had been spoken to him in near panic the night Magnus fell to the Priests of the Holy Grail.

He had been hidden in a stable while his castle fell—saved from death only because he was disguised as a beggar.

As Thomas projected his mind backward, the smells and sounds returned as if he were there again. The pungent warmth of horses and hay, the stamping of restless hooves, the blanket of darkness, a tired, frightened old woman clutching his arm, and the messenger in front of him.

"M'lord," Tiny John blurted. "The priests appeared within the castle as if from the very walls! Like hordes of rats. They—"

"Robert of Uleran," Thomas interrupted with a leaden voice. He wanted to sit beside the old woman and, along with her, moan in low tones. "How did he die?"

"Die?"

"You informed me that he spoke his last words."

"Last words to me, m'lord. Guards were falling in all directions, slapping themselves as they fell! The priests claimed it was the hand of God, and for all to lay down their arms. It was then that Robert of Uleran pushed this puppy into my arms and told me to flee, told me to give you warning so that you do not return to the castle . . . "

No, it cannot be, Thomas told himself again. Yet the Druids had posed as those false priests of the Holy Grail, the Druids had mysteriously appeared within the castle—undoubtedly through the secret passages which, in his last hours there, Thomas had discovered riddled Magnus—and the Druids had somehow struck down the well-armed soldiers within.

Guards were falling in all directions, slapping themselves as they fell.

Yellow-eye had slapped himself, then fallen.

Impossible that a Druid was aboard this same ship. Yet there was sense in such a rescue. Dead, Thomas would be worthless to to them. If only he knew how he had been followed, or who aboard was the Druid observer.

Thomas had little time to search or wonder. An hour later, a shout reached him from the watchtower at the top of the mast.

The port of Lisbon had been sighted.

2 0

To present myself as bait would be difficult under any circumstance, thought Thomas. *But to be bait without knowing the predator, and to be bait in a strange town with no idea where to spring and set the trap is sheer lunacy.*

Especially if that strange town is a danger in itself.

Lisbon sat at the mouth of the wide and slow River Tagus, a river deep enough to bring the ships in and out of the harbor area. The town itself was nestled between the river and two chains of hills rising on each side. It was one of the greatest shipping centers of Europe, for the Portuguese were some of the best sailors in the world.

Thomas stood at the end of a crowded street that led to the great docks of Lisbon. He leaned from one foot to the other, hoping to give an appearance of the uncertainty that he truly felt.

Which eyes follow me now?

Impossible to decide.

Hundreds upon hundreds, perhaps thousands of people

flooded the docks of Lisbon. Swaggering men of the sea, cackling hags, merchants pompously wrapped in fine silk, soldiers, bellowing fish sellers.

Sea gulls screamed and swooped. Wild and vicious cats, fat from fish offal, slunk from shadow to shadow. Rats, bold and large, scurried up or down the thick ropes which tethered ships to shore.

It was confusion driven by a single purpose. Greed. Those canny enough to survive the chaos—human or animal—also thrived in the chaos. Those who couldn't were often found in the forgotten corners of alleys, and never received a proper burial.

Thomas knew he needed to find such an alley, if only to finally expose his follower. And he only had a few hours of sunlight left. For he knew he would need the protection of a legion of angels should he be foolish enough to wander these corners of hell in the dark.

He moved forward, glad once again for the comfort of the puppy beneath his arm.

It took half of the remaining daylight to find the proper place for an ambush.

He had glanced behind him occasionally, only during the moments he pretended to examine a merchant's wares. Spices from Africa once, exquisite pottery from Rome another time, and strange objects of glass called spectacles which the bulky man with the too wide smile had assured him were the latest rage among highborn men and ladies all across Europe.

Not once had Thomas spotted a pursuer during those quick backward glances. Yet he dared not hope that meant he was alone or safe. Not after the strangeness of men collapsing because of an upraised sword.

Then, during his wanderings, he had noticed a side alley, leading away from the busy street. He walked through once and discovered it opened—after much twisting and turning—onto another busy street. The alley itself held many hidden doorways, already darkened by the late afternoon sun.

So Thomas circled, an action which cost him much of his precious time. In the maze of streets, it was no easy task to find the original entrance to the alley again.

Once inside that tiny corridor between ancient stone houses, Thomas smiled. Here, away from the bustle of the rest of the town, it was almost quiet. And, as with the first time through, it was empty of any passersby. He could safely assume any person who traveled through it behind him was his follower.

Thomas rounded a corner and slipped into a doorway.

He set the puppy down, and fumbled through his travel pouch for a piece of dried meat, then set that on the cobblestone.

"Chew on that, you little monster," Thomas whispered. "I have no need for your untimely interference again."

The puppy sat on his hindquarters and happily attacked the dried meat in silence.

Will it be flight or fight? Thomas wondered. His heart hammered against his ribs as each second passed. He knew he was well hidden in the shadows of the doorway. He could choose to let the follower move on and in turn stalk the stalker, or he could step out and challenge his unknown pursuer. *Which will it be?*

More seconds passed, each measured by several rapid beats of his heart.

Puppy remained silent.

Thomas did not hear footsteps. Rather, his pursuer moved along the cobblestone so quietly, that only the long shadow of afternoon sun behind him hinted at his arrival.

When the figure appeared in sight, head and neck straining ahead to see Thomas, the decision came instantly.

Fight.

For the figure was barely the size of a boy.

Thomas reached out and grasped for the shoulder of the small figure.

Reaction was so quick, that Thomas only managed a handful of cloth as that figure spun away and sprinted forward.

But not before Thomas recognized the filthy face and hat.

The cook's assistant.

Thomas bolted from the doorway in pursuit.

The cook's assistant. Surely he is a mere messenger or spy. Yet his capture is my only link to his masters.

Thomas ignored the pain of his feet slamming against the hard and irregular cobblestone. He ducked and twisted through the corners of the tiny alley, gaining rapidly on the figure in front.

Behind Thomas sounded the frantic barking of the puppy farther behind as he joined in this wonderful game.

Thomas closed in, now near enough to hear the heaving of breath ahead.

Three steps. Two steps. A single step away. Now tackle!

Thomas dove and wrapped his arms around the cook's assistant. Together, they tumbled in a ball of arms and legs.

Get atop! Grasp those wrists! Prevent the reaching for a dagger.

Thomas fought and scrambled, surprised at the wild strength of this smaller figure. For a moment, he managed to sit squarely on his opponent's stomach. A convulsive buck threw him off and Thomas landed dazed.

The cook's assistant scuttled sideways, but Thomas managed to roll over and reach around his waist and pull him back close into his body.

Then Thomas froze.

This is not what I should expect from a cook's assistant. Not a yielding softness of body that is more like . . .

Angry words from this mute cook's assistant interrupted his amazement and confirmed his suspicion.

. . . more like that of a woman.

"Unhand me, you murderous traitor."

It was the voice of Katherine.

Thomas scrambled to his feet and grabbed her wrist to help her upward.

She slapped his hand away, and reached her feet with a grace that made Thomas feel awkward.

Even without the hat that had always cast shade over her face aboard the ship, those layers of dirt, and that filthy hair cropped short, still made it difficult to recognize her, yet it truly was Katherine.

She glared hatred at him and spat on the ground beside him.

Yes, it is her indeed.

The puppy skidded to a halt between them.

Thomas barely noticed.

"You . . . what the . . . how . . ."

He did not finish his stammered sentence.

Katherine looked over his shoulder and her eyes widened.

There was a slight rustle and the sound of rushing air. Then a terrible black pain overwhelmed him.

When he woke, it only took several seconds to realize he was in a crude jail. Alone.

21

Thomas groaned aloud. He touched the back of his head—a foolish move, for he already knew how badly it ached, and his gentle probing of a large lump brought renewed stabs of pain.

That it was a jail around him, he had no doubt.

Early evening light filtered through a tiny square hole hewn through the stone.

The dimming light showed a straw-littered floor, stone walls worn smooth with time, so confining that he could touch all four easily from the center of the cell, and a battered wooden door.

Thomas stood, and groaned again.

He felt an incredible thirst, and staggered to the door. He thumped it weakly.

What evil has befallen me now?

As he waited for a response, he puzzled over this turn of events. *Who has thrown me here? Why? Did that devil's child Katherine have others to help?*

There was no answer, so Thomas thumped the door again.

The impact of the heel of his hand against wood worsened the throbbing of his head.

My cloak. My gold. My sword and sheath. Gone.

It finally dawned on Thomas that he had been stripped down to his undergarments.

In anger, he pounded the door again.

"Release me," he croaked through a parched throat. "Return my belongings."

Faint footsteps outside the door reached him as the echoes of his words faded in the twilight of his cell.

Then, a slight scraping of wood against wood as a someone outside slid back the cover of a small partition high in the door.

"Your majesty," a cackling voice called in sarcastic English heavily accented with thickened Portuguese vowels. "Come closer."

Thomas did.

"Do you stand before the door?" that voice queried. "Beneath the window?"

Thomas looked directly above him at the hole in the door which permitted the voice to float clearly through.

"Yes," Thomas answered.

"Good. Here's something to shut your mouth for the night."

Without warning, a cascade of filthy water arched through the opening. Drenched thoroughly, Thomas could only sputter.

"And I've got buckets more if *that* doesn't instruct you on manners. Now let me sleep."

The partition slammed shut, and footsteps outside retreated.

Thomas moved back to the side of his cell and gathered straw around him. Already he was beginning to shiver.

Shortly after the first star appeared in the small, square patch of sky that Thomas could see from his huddled position, across his feet ran the first rat of many in a long, sleepless night.

"Your majesty has a visitor." That heavy Portuguese accent interrupted Thomas' dreams.

Thomas opened gritty eyes to look upward at the face of a wrinkled gnome. A toothless grin leered down at him.

"Why should you enjoy sleep?" the voice continued.

Thomas began to focus, and the ancient gnome became an old tiny man with blackened gums that smacked and slobbered each word. "If I'm to be wakened this early, so must you."

The gnome-like man pointed back over his shoulder at the open doorway. "Why a common thief like you would receive such a visitor is beyond any mortal's understanding."

The gnome rattled on and touched Thomas' garments. "Dry," he said with disappointment. "Did I aim that slop so poorly last eve?"

Thomas ignored the man. And ignored the constant throbbing of his head, the itching of straw and flea bites, and the thirst that squeezed his throat.

He was transfixed by his visitor.

Katherine.

Not the Katherine he had seen in any form before. Not the Katherine as a noble friend, disguised as a freak in the wrapping of bandages. Not as the Katherine whose long blond hair had flowed in the moonlight during her visits as a midnight messenger. Not the Katherine who had betrayed him first to the Druids, then the outlaws. Not the Katherine covered with grime as a cook's assistant.

Thomas gaped at the transformation.

Gone was the filth. Gone were the rags.

Instead, a long cape of fine silk almost reached her feet. Holding the cloak in place was an oval clasp, showing a sword en-

graved into fine metal. Her neck and wrists glittered with exquisite jewelry. Her hair—still short—had been trimmed and al-
tered to highlight the delicate curves of her cheekbones.

A slight smile played across Katherine's face, as if she knew
his thoughts.

She would put a queen to shame.

Thomas fought against the surge of warmth that struck him at
that mysterious and aloof smile.

She is one of them, he warned himself, *one of the Druids who have
taken Magnus.*

He opened his mouth to speak, and she shook her head
slightly to caution him against it.

"This most certainly is my runaway servant," she said sternly.
"I shall see he is whipped thoroughly."

Servant?

The gnome-like man nodded with understanding. "Feed them
and clothe them and still they show no gratitude."

Servant?

"I have spoken to the authorities," Katherine continued. "The
boy that this—" Katherine sniffed scorn and pointed at Thomas
"—scoundrel attacked has not reappeared to seek compensa-
tion. Given that, and the fortune in gold that changed from my
hands to the magistrate's, I have been granted permission for
his return."

The gnome-like man somehow shook his head in sympathy.
"Is he worth this?"

"A promise to his mother, a long-time servant," Katherine
answered. "She was dear to our family, and we vowed never to
let her son stray."

"Aaah," the jailer said.

He kicked Thomas. "Be sure we don't see your face again."

Thomas pushed himself to his feet. His back felt like a board
from leaning against the cold stone, his legs ached from shiver-

ing, and his head still throbbed. *Now he was to be treated as her servant?*

Yet, what were his alternatives?

He shuffled forward meekly.

Wait, he promised himself, *until she and I are away from listening ears.*

Not until the jailer retrieved Thomas' outer garments did he realize how immodest it was to be standing there in his undergarments. He seethed with frustration as he dressed—stumbling awkwardly as he balanced on one leg, then the next—under her smirking gaze.

Then Thomas followed her through the narrow corridor—not daring to wonder what poor souls wasted away behind the other silent wooden prison doors—into the bright sunlight outside.

They stood at the north end of the harbor, and the noise and confusion of the chaos of men busy among ships reached them clearly.

"You were arrested yesterday," Katherine began, "as you lay there gasping like a stunned fish."

Thomas rubbed the back of his head. "What foul luck. Certainly a harbor like this has only a handful of men who guard and patrol for the townspeople."

"He was pleased to be such a hero," Katherine said. "Rarely do such bold crimes occur in broad daylight. He also seemed pleased at the accuracy of his blow."

She paused. "It cost fully a quarter of your gold to pay your ransom."

"*My* gold?" Thomas sputtered.

"Of course," Katherine said calmly. "I lifted your pouch as I helped them drag you away."

"*My* gold?"

"Had I not, the jailer certainly would have. After all, did he not keep your sword and sheath?"

Thomas ground his teeth in anger.

"Fear not," Katherine said sweetly. "As the cook's assistant, I spirited away your puppy. It remains safely waiting for you at the inn."

"And my remaining gold?" Thomas spat each word.

Her voice remained sweet. "Much of it purchased this fine clothing. I needed to pose as a noblewoman retrieving an errant servant. Besides, it would serve neither of us for me to remain as a mere shiphand on our next voyage."

"*Much* of it? *Next* voyage?" He caught the implications. "*Our* next voyage?"

"Yes."

"Hardly," Thomas vowed. "I have my own path to follow."

"Not unless you jump ship," Katherine said smugly. "I need only say the word and you will be thrown in jail again. Until we leave Lisbon, you are mine, and under my orders, you will board the ship of my choice."

"You have much to explain." Thomas now dared not trust himself to say more. His fists were clenched in fury.

"Perhaps. But as my penniless servant, you are in no position to dictate any terms."

She favored him with another radiant smile.

"And my first command is that you bathe. You smell wretched."

"You should find the servants' quarters somewhere below," Katherine said as they stepped onto the gangway.

Thomas gritted his teeth. Katherine had been shrewd enough to dispense an amount of gold that guaranteed eternal loyalty from the port authorities.

Twice, in fact, he had rebelled during this long day since his release from prison. Was it not bad enough she had refused to return to him his remaining gold? Was it not bad enough she had taken such enjoyment at his discomfort — before and after his time in the public bath? Twice he had stormed from her, uncaring that he was penniless in a strange town. And twice he had been overtaken by a pair of guards who offered him the alternative of jail or a return to his master, that wonderful noblewoman.

So now he stood on the gangway that led to the galley *Santa Magdellen,* an Italian merchant galley. This ship, unlike the *Dragon's Eye's* single mast with square sail, had two masts with *lateens*—triangular sails—which, in the calmer seas of the mid

Atlantic and Mediterranean, enabled the ship to sail into winds with a minimum of tacking back and forth.

Thomas scowled at Katherine. But discreetly. He could see lurking behind her on the dock the two guards, and remembered they had not been gentle in the manner in which they had persuaded him both times earlier to return to her instead of jail.

She smiled back. Sweetly, of course.

He wanted to stitch her lips together, anything to rid her of that assured smile. He wanted to shake her by the shoulders and loosen the words from her mouth, words to explain how she had followed him, and how she had known his destination, to find passage on a galley which sailed to Israel, the Holy Land. And—far worse—he wanted to be able to stare into those taunting blue eyes for every heartbeat of the rest of his life.

That confusion only served to deepen his foul mood.

She is one of them, he forced himself to remember each time their eyes met. *I should not feel this insane warmth.*

So he growled surly agreement at her directions to the servants' area, and began to march to the cramped and foul area of the ship which would be his home for several weeks.

"Thomas," she called before he took three steps.

He turned around and scowled again.

She pointed to the expensive leather bags at her feet which held her considerable array of travel possessions—all purchased with his gold. One of the bags held the smuggled puppy. Neither wanted trouble with this crew.

"Must you forget the simplest of duties?" Katherine asked. "Surely you don't expect *me* to carry these bags to my quarters."

It took nearly an hour to leave the harbor. The galley was awkward at slow speeds, and the ship's captain dared not raise the sails until they reached the open sea.

The crew used oars instead; Thomas was half surprised that Katherine had not volunteered his services as an oarsman.

In the hum of activity of departure, Thomas easily moved unnoticed to the prow of the ship where Katherine stood and enjoyed the breeze above the water.

Spray cascaded against the wooden bow as the galley rose and fell with the waves. That sound made it easy from him to approach her back without being heard.

"Have I not been tortured enough?" he asked. He was tall enough that he had to bend to speak the words into her ear.

She half turned and stepped back, not startled—or refusing to show surprise—at his sudden presence. "I've hardly begun," she said. "But this is a long voyage and I remember well your treatment of me as I hung by a rope."

"Do not hold those foolish dreams of revenge," Thomas said. "We are away from those wretched Lisbon watchdogs. I shall be my own man now."

She smiled. "If you glance over your shoulder, you will see unfriendly eyes watching closely your every move."

Thomas groaned. "Not so."

"Indeed," Katherine informed him. "Your gold has proven to work wonders with the ship's captain as well. He has promised to have you whipped should you exhibit the same behavior which jailed you in Lisbon."

"My gold cannot last for eternity," Thomas protested. "Silks, perfumes, rich food, passage, and now protection! I had planned to live for a year on that gold."

"Wool," Katherine said.

"Wool?" Thomas stared at her as if she had lost her sanity.

"Silks, perfumes, rich food, passage, protection. And wool."

"Wool?" The despair of comprehension began to fill his voice.

"Wool," she repeated patiently. "This merchant ship holds twenty tons of wool which I purchased with your gold. Even after the price of passage, I should profit handsomely with its sale when we arrive in the Holy Land.

"Impossible," Thomas said through lips thinned with frustration.

"Oh no," Katherine assured him. "Wool is much needed in far ports."

"I . . . meant . . . impossible . . . that . . . I . . . had . . . enough . . . gold . . . for . . . twenty . . . tons . . . of . . . wool." Thomas could hardly speak now, so difficult was it to remain in control.

Katherine dismissed that with a cheerful wave. "Had I neglected to inform you that I borrowed heavily from the supply of gold you have hidden in England?"

His mouth dropped.

"Remember?" she prompted. "Near the cave which contains your secret books?"

A strangled gasp left his throat. Thomas clutched his chest.

"It was child's play to follow you to Scarborough after your contest with the outlaw Robert Hood. All I needed to do was return to that cave and wait for your arrival."

She lifted an eyebrow and pretended surprise. "You expected that I would remain with the outlaws to share the ransom collected for Isabelle?"

Thomas closed his eyes briefly, as if fighting a spasm of pain.

"Thomas, Thomas," she chided. "Surely you don't believe it was your doing to win the contest with the outlaw?"

His eyes now widened.

"Robert Hood had been told to lose. I wanted you set free." She moved closer to him and mockingly placed a consoling hand on his arm. "Take comfort, however. He admitted later the outcome was not certain, even had he wanted to defeat you."

Thomas slapped her hand away.

"Woman," he said fiercely. "You have pushed me too far."

He grew cold with rage as he continued. "My fight for Magnus was a deathbed promise to the nurse who raised and loved me more than my parents might ever had done. Every pain suffered to fulfill that pledge is a pain I would gladly have suffered ten times over."

He stepped closer—now controlled in anger—but did not raise his voice.

"Yet even after victory, the strange secrets behind Magnus haunted me. And each new secret I've glimpsed has had your face. I fight enemies I cannot see, and I fight enemies I wish I could not see. Too many good men have sacrificed themselves for this fight."

He advanced while she backed to the railing.

"Yet the reason for this fight—a reason I am certain you know—has been kept from me. And even the reason it has been kept from me has been kept from me."

He paused for breath. "Your face and those secrets follow me here to the ends of the earth. And now I am your prisoner on a tiny ship in vast waters. You have stolen my gold. You have humiliated me."

He raised his forefinger and held it beneath her chin. "And now you mock me in tone and words. I will take no more."

Thomas stepped back and said in a whisper. "From this moment on, wherever you stand on this boat, I will choose the point farthest away from you. Threaten me, punish me, have me thrown overboard. I do not care. For I wash my hands of you."

He stared at her for a long moment, then let scorn fill his face before turning away.

She called to his back immediately.

"Forgive me," Katherine said. The mocking banter in her voice had disappeared. "Love leads one to do strange things."

"**Que je ne** peux pas *ne pas* t'aimer," Katherine said.

Thomas was still stunned by her first words. So it took his befuddled brain a moment to translate.

"I cannot *not* love you," she had said.

Why French?

"And I have loved you fiercely since I was a child," she said.

Although he understood those words clearly, it took Thomas another moment to realize her last sentence had been spoken in faultless German.

Since she was a child?

"I see by the light in your eyes," Katherine said, now in English, "that you understand well my words. And that is part of why I cannot not love you."

"Truth and answers," Thomas replied, using Latin. "Only a fool would throw away love offered by you, but first I need truth and answers."

She smiled at his switch in language, and answered him in Latin.

"Have we not received the same education? Have we not been driven mercilessly by our teachers to be literate and fluent in all the civilized languages when few in this world can even read in their own tongue?"

She moved to Thomas again, and placed again her hand on his forearm. This touch, however, was tender, not mocking. "And have we not been trained to fight the same fight against the same enemies?"

She looked beyond Thomas, and discreetly removed her hand from his arm. "The ship's captain approaches. Tonight, we talk."

The five hours until moonlight seemed to take as long as the entire voyage from England to Lisbon. Thomas had stood on the stern platform, staring at the coastline directly eastward that became little more than a faint haze with distance. His only consolation during the long wait was that seasickness had not struck again.

I dare not trust her, he had told himself again and again. *Her vow of love is merely a trick. For if she were not one of them, how else could I have been captured in my camp the morning after her arrival with the old man?*

Yet, the old man had spoken of Merlins — raised from birth to fight the evil spawned by generations of a secret society of Druids. I had almost believed him — until my capture through their betrayal.

And yet I must consider also the alternative. If Katherine is a Merlin — and can truly explain the apparent betrayal — she is my only hope to recapture Magnus, my source to the secrets which have plagued me.

So I must pretend to believe her. And refuse to let my heart be fooled as it so desperately wants.

Thomas remained on the stern platform all those hours until she appeared.

Her hair was now silver in the moonlight, her face a haunting mixture of shadows.

I cannot read her eyes. How do I dare trust her words?

"You know by now that a secret war rages," she began without a greeting. "Druids, who have chosen darkness and secrecy as the way to power. And Merlins, who battle back in equal secrecy."

Thomas nodded.

"You and I were born to Merlin parents," Katherine said. "But not even birth destines a child to be a Merlin. Many, in fact, live and grow old unaware of their parents' mission."

Thomas held up a hand to interrupt.

"Certainly I know of the Druids," he said. "Their circle of evil is ancient. The Roman Emperor Julius Caesar observed them more than twelve hundred years ago, when they still reigned openly in Britain."

Katherine nodded. "Of course. You know that from your books in the cave. But of Merlins—"

"Of Merlins I know nothing more than their name, as mentioned by the old man and another I knew in Magnus. It is more than passing strange they—we—bear the same name of King Arthur's wise man and trusted counselor."

"More than passing strange," Katherine agreed. "King Arthur and his Knights ruled some hundreds of years after the Roman conquerors had taken Britain and forced the Druids into hiding openly."

"Hidden openly?"

"Openly. The safest way to hide. Blacksmiths, tanners, farmers, noblemen, knights, priests during the day. But at night . . . " Katherine's voice trailed. "At night they would meet to continue their quest for power."

She shivered, although the night air was warm. "Frightening, is it not? Any man or woman you might meet in England—a false sorcerer at night. And many strove for positions of power in open society, the better to influence the direction of their secret plans."

Thomas spat disgust, but said nothing. He knew too well the treachery of Druids.

"Merlin?" he prompted her.

"Yes. Merlin. Eight hundred years ago. The brightest and best of the Druids."

Thomas stood transfixed. The creaking of the ship, the passing of water, the clouds slipping past the moon, he was aware of none of it.

"Merlin, a Druid?" he asked.

"It explains much, does it not? His powers have become legendary—some call him an enchanter. Equipped with the knowledge of a Druid—knowledge that is considerable and often seems magic to poor, ignorant peasants—he accomplished much through deception. And what better place for a Druid than at the right hand of Britain's finest king?"

Thomas shook his head, trying to understand. "Yet he battled. . . ."

"Yet Merlin battled the same Druids who raised him to such power."

"Why?" Thomas asked softly. He let his mind drift back those eight hundred years to the court of King Arthur—Sir Galahad, Sir Lancelot, and the other Knights of the Round Table. And Merlin, the man who established that Round Table, at the right hand of Britain's most powerful man. "Merlin had everything a man might desire. Why risk losing all by rejecting the same Druids who had given him that power?"

"It is legend among us," Katherine said equally softly. "The Druids had waited generations for one of them to have the power that Merlin did. Finally, there was one to set into motion the plan that would let them conquer the entire kingdom, a plan so evil that its success would establish the Druids forever. Merlin was the one man able to ensure success. And he became the one man to stop them. The legend is that a simple priest showed Merlin the power of faith in God by—"

"A bold plan to establish the Druids?" Thomas interrupted. "More established than they are now? More power than they have as a circle unknown and hidden among the people?"

"Yes," she said. "A plan great and terrible. Our own legends tell us the horror of it led Merlin to seek the simple priest, led him to the decision to end the Druids' quest for power, and led him to his vow that they might never make another attempt at such a plan again. Merlin founded generations of the Druids' greatest enemies, each person equipped with the knowledge of a Druid. In short, he turned their own powerful sword upon themselves. Since then, we have fought them—generation by generation—at every turn. We have held them at bay. Until now."

"What is at the end of this evil plan?" Thomas asked.

Hesitation. Then Katherine said, "I do not know. The old man always promised to tell me. But never had that chance."

Does she lie? Or are her faltering words because of grief for the old man?

Thomas paced back and forth several times, then asked. "The Merlins also hide openly?"

"Yes."

"And seek positions of power to counteract the influence of Druids?"

"Yes." Katherine smiled. "Sometimes we reach fame through these efforts. And we reach far. Generations ago, Charles the Great, King of the Franks, sent for educated people from all over Christendom. He wanted his people to learn again, from books."

Katherine paused, trying to recall the story. "The Druids had arranged to send one of them there. What better way to spread evil in other countries? We intercepted the orders and replaced that Druid with a man named Alcuin. He rose quickly within the royal court of the Franks, and did untold good, spreading knowledge and even introducing a new style of writing."

She waved her hand. "There are others of course, through the ages. We have all been taught the stories of our history."

Thomas frowned. "How many of us are there?"

Katherine sighed. "Before Magnus fell twenty years ago, hundreds. More than enough to keep the Druids from reaching their goal."

"And now?"

"I . . . I . . . do not know. I have only the stories that the old man taught me."

She became quiet, the memory of the old man too hard to bear.

Thomas sensed her sadness, and tried to occupy her with other thoughts. "Hundreds? How could hundreds be taught in secrecy. That would take hundreds of teachers!"

"Not so," Katherine replied, her voice not entirely free of sorrow. "Merlin devised a new method. He appointed his successor before he died. And each successor appointed another, so that Merlin's command was passed directly from generation to generation. Each leader was the finest among us and selected teachers, who each generation shared knowledge with entire groups who sat together. One teacher had as many as thirty listeners."

Thomas whistled appreciation. " 'Tis wondrous strange. Yet seems so simple. Now it strikes me odd this method is not followed elsewhere."

Katherine nodded. "Merlin called it 'school.' "

Thomas stumbled over the strange word. "School."

Katherine nodded again. "Our legends tell us he so named it

because schools of fish reminded him of the way we gather to listen, but this I must believe is a story invented for only the youngest Merlins."

Thomas barely heard her last words. Much now made sense.

Magnus. Isolated in the moors north of England, far from the intrigues and attention of reigning monarchs.

Magnus. With only moderate wealth, not a prize worth seeking.

Magnus. Insignificant, nearly invisible.

Magnus. Hidden as it was, with the largest fortress in the north, a construction which must have cost a king's ransom, far more than the land itself could earn, even with the profit of centuries of income.

Magnus. Hidden as it was, with the largest fortress in the north, yet with seemingly nothing to protect.

Magnus. Riddled with secret passageways.

Thomas understood. He stopped pacing abruptly and voiced his certainty to Katherine.

"Merlin established Magnus. Obscure and well protected, it has been the training ground for every generation who followed."

"Yes," she said. "Merlin chose Magnus, and had the fortress built. He retired to the island in that remote land. From there, he taught the others and sent them throughout the country to combat the Druids in hidden warfare. And Magnus served us well for hundreds of years. Even after the Druids finally discovered its location and purpose, it took generations for them to conquer it. I was not there when that happened, of course, but the old man told me that their surprise attack and ruthless slaughter twenty years ago all but destroyed the Merlins. Only a few survived."

She stopped, and in the dim light, Thomas could see she was trying to search his face.

"And Thomas," she finally whispered, "you were appointed shortly after your birth, chosen as Merlin's successor of this generation to reconquer Magnus for us."

2 4

Thomas stood and squarely faced her, with feet braced and arms crossed. It was the only way he could stop the trembling which threatened to overwhelm him.

I want so badly to believe her.

"You weave a fanciful tale," he said scornfully. "Yet if it were true, why was I not told of this?"

"But you were, in a way," Katherine said softly. "Was it an accident you were hidden in that obscure abbey? Was it an accident that Sarah, your childhood nurse, gladly exiled herself there to raise and train you as thoroughly as if you had been raised in Magnus as son of the reigning earl?"

That startled Thomas into dropping his bluff of indifference.

"You jest! My father was a mason, a builder of churches. He and my mother died of the plague, and left behind money to pay for my education among the clergy."

"No, Thomas. Sarah had been commanded to keep the truth from you. Your father, the ruler of Magnus, was the appointed leader of *his* generation of Merlins. It was too important that no one ever discover your real identity, and it was feared that as a child, you might blurt it aloud in front of the wrong ears."

Thomas shook his head. "Sarah encouraged me to dream of reigning over Magnus, but she always told me it was *her* parents I should avenge."

Katherine disagreed, sadly. "Too many of the Merlins fell with Magnus. The old man often told me you were our only hope, that should the Druids discover the only son of the last leader of the Merlins was still alive, they would leave no stone in England unturned in their search to have you murdered."

Thomas took several moments to consider this staggering news. "My father reigned over Magnus? My father was the successor to Merlin? It was my father's death at the Druid hands that I was raised to avenge?"

"Yes."

Thomas raised his hands helplessly. "I should have been told this. I stumbled in the darkness." His voice became accusing. "Alone."

Katherine put a finger to her own lips to silence his protests. "How old were you when Sarah died?"

"Nine."

"Too young to be trusted yet with that precious knowledge. And there was no one who could replace her at the abbey to instruct you more. The old man often told me that we could only trust her training had been a magnificent seed, that you would learn more from the books left with you, and that you would always remember Magnus."

Thomas shook his head again, more firmly. "Yet I ruled Magnus for three seasons. Neither you, nor the old man, nor Gervase revealed this to me then."

Katherine moved to the edge of the ship and stared away. Thomas was forced to follow to be able to listen to her words before they were swallowed by the breeze.

"We could not," she said, still staring at the moon. "For you had been alone at the abbey for five years. We could not know if the Druids had found you and claimed you as one of their own."

"I conquered Magnus! I took it from them!"

Katherine sighed. "Yes. I argued that often with the old man. He told me that we played a terrible game of chess against unseen masters. He told me they might have artfully arranged a simple deception, that the more it seemed you were against them, the more likely we might be to tell you the final truth, and in so doing, lose this centuries old battle in the quickest of heartbeats."

Thomas pondered her words and spoke slowly. "What is the final truth?"

The constant splash of water against the side of the galley was his only reply.

"The final truth," he demanded.

"Not even I was told."

She lies. I can sense that, even with her face turned away from me. Yet, I must pretend to believe.

So Thomas said, "There is an undeniable logic in that. How could you *ever* finally believe that I was not a Druid, posing as one of you. So I was watched. By Gervase, who posed as a simple old caretaker. And by you, in your disguise beneath the bandages."

"I am relieved you understand."

There is a simple flaw with this entire story. And it breaks my heart. Yet I cannot leave it lie.

So Thomas spun her to face him and squeezed both her wrists without mercy.

"But explain," he said fiercely, "why you finally tell me all this now. And explain it well, or I shall cast you overboard."

2 5

"No, Thomas," she begged. "You must let go!"

His response was to pull her closer to the edge of the ship. *She must believe this terrible bluff.*

Thomas had no chance to continue it.

"Speak now—" he started.

Her eyes widened and she called out, "No!"

But her cry was not directed at Thomas.

He heard a scuffling of feet, and began to turn his head. *Late, much too late.* A familiar blackness crashed down upon him.

Thomas dreamed that gigantic court jesters juggled him like a tiny ball, laughing and yelling as they tossed him back and forth.

He woke with a muffled shout just as the most hideous jester dropped him, and discovered indeed he had been tossed back and forth, but in the confines of the brig in the belly of the ship.

Thomas propped out a hand to keep from pitching back to the other side, and waited for his eyes to adjust to the dimness. The extent of his new prison—walls of rough wood and iron bars for a door—made the cell in Lisbon seem like a castle.

His head felt it might split.

Uncanny, he thought with a twisted grin, *they managed to hit me in the exact spot of my previous lump. Do bumps grow atop bumps?*

He was able to contemplate this imprisonment for several hours before he had a visitor.

"No," he groaned at the scent of perfume, "curse me with your arrival no longer."

"Hush," Katherine said. "I risk too much even now. A real noblewoman saved from the attack of a rebellious servant would never grace him with a visit."

Thomas shook his head slightly, but at the reverberations of pain, held it very still. "You had us watched as we spoke," he accused. "And they believed I would harm you."

"Would you?" Katherine asked.

"Then, no." He touched the back of his head. "Now, yes."

She smiled. "I have little time. Yet I want to answer your question."

Thomas studied her face through the iron bars.

"In Scarborough," Katherine began, "you made an error. You sought advice from an old hag who sold fish, advice on how to reach the Holy Land."

Thomas shrugged, then winced. "Unfamiliar with the ways of the sea, I needed that advice. And I dared not ask any ship captain. I did not want him to know my destination. So I asked her, thinking she would never remember a passing stranger."

"A passing stranger with a tail sticking out of his cloak as he walked away?"

"The puppy."

"Yes," Katherine said. "Now safely hidden in my quarters.

Thus I discovered your destination. There was only one ship in the harbor leaving for Lisbon. It was not difficult to sign on as a cook's assistant."

"Why—"

"Hush. Time flees too quickly."

She took a breath. "I had intended merely to follow you on both ships. Until you lured me into the trap and had the misfortune to be arrested." She stopped, puzzled. "How was it you guessed you had been followed aboard the ship?"

"The manner in which three hardened sailors fell at the wave of my sword. It was the same mysterious manner in which my soldiers fell at Magnus."

Katherine giggled. "The surprise on your face as they fell!" Then she sobered. "A Druid trick. Short, thick, hollow straws. A puff of breath directs a tiny pellet coated with a sleeping potion. I was in the shadows nearby, watching because I had heard the crewmen speak, and knew you were in danger."

A Druid trick. Either she tells the truth and is a Merlin who knows much about the enemy. Or she is the enemy. How do I decide?

Thomas nodded to conceal his doubt. "Why reveal what you did last night? Why now if not ever before?"

"I will tell you now. And there is no need to threaten to throw me overboard," Katherine replied. "When you were arrested, desperate measures were needed. I had to help you out, and could only do so by playing the role I did. As a noblewoman. And by then, I had also decided you were not a Druid. Not if you were truly going to the Holy Land by yourself."

She hesitates. What does she hide?

Katherine must have caught the doubt in his eyes. "The old man is gone. If you were a Merlin, I needed your help as badly as you needed mine. It was a risk worth taking. If you are a Druid . . . I knew I was safe, protected by your gold as a noblewoman there in Lisbon, and here on the ship."

Perhaps. But there must be more. It is obvious in her manner.

Thomas nodded in pretend satisfaction.

He thrust his hands through the gap between the iron bars and spoke softly.

"Love," he said. "Since childhood?"

She took his hands in hers. Although he had meant it as an appearance of trust, the touch of her hands in his filled him with warmth.

Do not trust her, nor your heart. Yet remember the first time you met her, and how there had been an instinctive reaching of your heart for hers, as if it was remembering a love deeply buried.

And he could not ignore the happiness that swelled his throat.

"Love. Since childhood and before you arrived at Magnus," she repeated. "I pray in the Holy Land that much more will be revealed to both of us."

A noise from behind startled her into dropping both his hands.

"Thomas," she said quickly. "If it is possible to return safely, I will. Otherwise . . ."

She picked up the ends of her long cape, and disappeared in the opposite direction of an approaching crewman.

Thomas did not see her until the galley reached the harbor of St. Jean d'Acre, the last city of the Crusaders in the Holy Land to fall to the Muslim infidels.

26

Two crewmen brought Thomas to the deck of the ship as summoned by Katherine. He needed the help given by their rough hands which grasped his upper arms to keep him upright. Not only was he weak from the lack of proper food, but the brig had been so cramped, his legs were no longer accustomed to bearing his weight. And his ankles were now shackled by chains of iron.

The crewman left him beside Katherine and waited watchfully nearby.

She remained silent. It would serve neither of them if she appeared anything but the vengeful noblewoman.

Thomas stared past her at the half-ruined towers—still magnificent—rising from the land at the edge of waters of the Mediterranean Sea.

St. Jean d'Acre was a town on a peninsula surrounded almost entirely by sea. Once—when still in Christian hands—it had been protected by a massive wall that ran across the peninsula, so that the only approach for attack was by water. Thomas knew from the hurried reading in his books that Acre was also the last Christian city to fall to the Muslims, barely twenty years earlier, in the year A.D. 1291 when the last of the Crusaders had finally been defeated after 200 years of war in the Holy Land.

Acre was one mile west of the ancient inland towns of Akka and Accho, 20 miles northwest of Nazareth, and 70 miles northwest of the Holy City, Jerusalem. He felt an anticipation of excitement to think of the Holy City, sought so often by the Crusaders of the past.

The air around him was steamy hot—a heat he had never felt before. The sun seemed much larger than he remembered of the sun in England, and its glare was an attack of fury. The buildings that shimmered before his eyes as the galley grew closer were formed in unfamiliar, sharply rounded curves.

At that moment—despite the heat—Thomas felt a chill replace his anticipation.

This land is so foreign, I am doomed before I begin. Muslims have fought Christians here for centuries, and I step onto their land, not even able to . . .

Thomas took a deep breath as that new thought almost staggered him.

I have been so intent on reaching the Holy Land, I have overlooked the single most obvious barrier to my success here. I do not speak the language!

He wanted badly to discuss this with Katherine, but as he shuffled sideways to whisper his concern, the ship's captain approached.

He was a great bear of a man with swarthy skin and a hooked nose. Curiously, he wore a purple turban.

"M'lady," he said respectfully, "you have informed us, of course, that you are here to seek relatives. We all wish you Godspeed in the search. Many fine families lost sons here during the Crusades—dead, injured perhaps, or missing. Rumors do reach us of surviving knights still alive among the *infidels.*

Perhaps your mission will be blessed."

He paused, searching for a delicate way to impart advice. "This is a strange land with strange customs. Men . . . men take insult if a woman shows her face. To be sure, you will have no difficulty finding a buyer for your wool. Yet you must wear this at all times in public, including the times you negotiate with merchants."

The ship's captain held out a black veil.

Katherine slipped it over her head. It stopped short of the clasp at her neck which held her cloak together.

"You have my gratitude," Katherine told the ship's captain. "Would that all I might meet have the grace and kindness which you have extended me."

He bowed slightly, then frowned at Thomas. "Shall we whip him once to ensure meekness ashore?"

Katherine removed the veil, held it in her left hand, and touched her chin with the tip of her right forefinger as she studied Thomas. A mischievous glint escaped her eyes.

"No," she said finally. "I think the shackles should suffice."

Thomas, unshackled now that they were clear of the galley, could hardly believe his ears.

He stood with Katherine in the crowded *fonduk*, a large open-square warehouse on the eastern waterfront. It had belonged to the Venetians before Acre fell to the Muslims. Now, as the best trading area in a town where major trading routes met the sea, it was occupied by hundreds of sharp-eyed Arab merchants.

He stood amazed for one simple reason. The clamoring babble which surrounded him made sense.

"Don't trust his olive oil," one shout reached him clearly. "That merchant is as crooked as a snake's path!"

"Here for the finest salt!" another voice shouted.

"Silk from the overland journeys!" "Camels for hire!"

Each fragment of excited conversation filtered through his mind.

He understood each word!

And Katherine stood in front of him, face hidden modestly by her veil, bartering over the price of wool with an eager merchant.

In their language!

How could this be?

He stood and watched the chaos around him with an open mouth. The harbor area of Lisbon now seemed like a sleepy town in comparison.

Camels, donkeys, and gesturing men in long white sheets and turbans in all directions. Strange animals with long slender tails — could these be the monkeys of which he had read? Finely woven carpets, baskets as tall as a man, beggars . . .

Katherine tugged on his arm.

"I have finished," she said in English. Satisfaction filled her words. "As predicted, I have doubled my investment."

"*Our* investment," Thomas felt the need to immediately correct her, although more pressing things engaged him.

He leaned forward.

"Their words!" he said. "I understand."

"As well you should," Katherine replied. "It is part of your child—"

A beggar darted up to her and chattered excitedly.

"Lady, lady, from where did you get such a fine clasp?"

Katherine reached for her neck and touched it in response. "I—"

"Very fine! Very fine!" the beggar interrupted. "I can find someone to give you an excellent price for it!"

"I am flattered, of course, yet—"

"Double what you had expected!" the beggar insisted. Then he stopped and looked at her coyly. "Or is it a family heirloom?"

Katherine nodded firmly from behind her veil. "It will never be sold."

Unexpectedly, the beggar darted away without another word.

"Strange," Thomas said. "About this childhood matter . . ."

"Of course," Katherine reassured him. "But first, we must purchase you clothing which lets you blend among these people. And a sword."

She giggled. "And once again, you are in dire need of time in a public bathhouse."

2 7

"I no longer feel half-dead," Thomas grinned. "A rest tonight in a bed that does not shift with the waves, some food, and I will be ready to conquer the world."

Katherine smiled back from behind her veil.

They gazed at each other in silence for several seconds, forming an island of privacy in the hectic motion of the market around them outside the bath house.

Don't let those eyes fool you. Remember, you will only remain with her until you discover the truths you need. There is nothing more to this situation.

To cover the flush he felt beneath her gaze, Thomas bantered and gestured at his robe and sword at his side. "Am I not the perfect infidel? Especially after you tell me how it is I understand their language."

"Perfect," Katherine agreed lightly. "We—"

She frowned.

"Thomas, to your left. Is it not the same beggar who approached me for this clasp?"

Thomas turned his head quickly enough to see the beggar grasping the sleeve of two large men and pointing in their direction.

"The same," Thomas confirmed.

All eyes locked across the space between them. The beggar and his companions, each armed with scimitars, those great curving swords. And Thomas and Katherine staring back at them in return.

"Do you find a startling resemblance between those two men and a pair of wolves?" Thomas asked softly without removing his eyes from them.

"Hungry wolves," Katherine said. "I like this not. We should return to the inn and see your puppy instead."

They backed away quickly. And soon discovered they were prey for the two large men.

In a half run, Katherine and Thomas darted around market stalls and through crowds of people.

"This way!" Katherine cried.

"No . . . " But Thomas did not protest in time. Katherine had already chosen a narrow alley.

Why have they chosen us? Thomas wondered as he ran. *Because we are foreign? Surely it cannot be because of the Druids. We have only just arrived.*

Thomas nearly stumbled on the street's uneven stones as he stopped and turned to run after her. His sword slapped against his side.

I pray I will not have to use this weapon, he thought, *these men are larger and stronger.*

The two men gained ground. They were familiar with the twists of the alley. Thomas and Katherine were not.

Each second brought the men closer and closer. Thomas and Katherine were now in a full run, slipping beneath archways and around blind corners.

"Again! This way!" Katherine panted. "We are nearly there!"

"No . . . " Thomas moaned. He did not know the town at all, but knew with certainty her path led them away both from the waterfront and from the inn.

Without warning, Katherine stopped and pounded on a door hidden in a recess in the alley.

"That is not the inn!" Thomas warned.

"Behind you!" Katherine said. She banged the door with her fist, while staring in horror at the approaching swordsmen.

Thomas did the only thing he could. He drew his sword.

Katherine pounded the door.

"You cannot avoid the assassins' pledge," the first man snarled as he lifted his scimitar.

Thomas managed to parry the first blow, then step aside as the other swung.

I have only seconds to live, he realized. *In cramped quarters, against those great swords, I might as well already be dead.*

"Katherine," he said quickly. "Run while you might."

In answer, he felt her presence plucked from his side.

The door has opened, he realized with the part of his mind that was not focused on survival.

Another whistling blow. Thomas met it with his own steel, and the echoing clank was almost as painful as the jar of contact that shivered up his arm.

Thomas brandished his sword and prepared for a counter-attack.

If I'm to die, they will pay the price.

Both men hesitated and stepped back.

"Cowards!" Thomas cried in the full heat of battle.

"No," came a strangely familiar voice from the very spot Katherine had stood only moments earlier. "They are simply prudent."

Both men stepped back farther.

"Yes," the voice continued, now directed at them. "This crossbow truly reaches farther and faster than the sword. Go back to the men who hired you. Tell them the blood they wish to spill is now under protection."

The swordsmen nodded, and quickly spun around, then hurried around the nearest corner of the alley.

Thomas, still panting, turned to look at his rescuer.

"Well, puppy," he was greeted. "Must we always meet in such troubled circumstances?"

Thomas only stared in return.

Sir William. The knight who helped me conquer Magnus. The knight who disappeared three seasons ago on his own private quest.

Thomas finally found his voice. "You describe harmless gnats like those two as trouble? Truly, you must be growing old."

Now, as when the knight had bid farewell long ago in Magnus, Thomas fought a lump in his throat.

Then, an early morning breeze had gently flapped the knight's colors against the stallion beneath him. Behind them both had been the walls of Magnus. Ahead of them had been the winding trail that had taken the knight to a destination he could not reveal.

This destination.

St. Jean d'Acre. On the edge of the Holy Land.

The sorrow Thomas felt in remembering their farewell mixed like a sweet wine with the sorrow of a renewed remembrance of Magnus.

He blinked back emotion.

Sir William smiled, switched the crossbow to his left hand, and extended his right hand in a clasp of greeting.

"Still one to watch and learn." The knight smiled again. "You did the same thing during our first encounter. Remember? As we fought over the log across that stream?"

Thomas smiled. For indeed, he was trying to absorb the details around him. Instead of the hills of Magnus, the worn stones of a doorway in a town nearly as ancient as mankind.

The knight had changed little. Still darkly tanned, hair still cropped short, now with a trace of gray at the edges. Blue eyes still as deep as they were careful to hide thoughts. And always, that ragged scar down his right cheek.

A sudden thought struck Thomas.

"You are one of us." Although it was a guess, Thomas spoke it as a statement. "A Merlin."

Sir William nodded. "And one unable to decide whether to be gladdened or sorrowful at your arrival in the fallen town of the Last Crusaders."

Thomas raised an eyebrow.

"That you are here speaks volumes of the dire trouble that faces Magnus," Sir William said.

Thomas nodded. Nothing could have prepared him for the words he heard next.

"Yet in this dark cloud exists more than a tiny part of joy." The knight paused and studied Thomas' face. "For one man has waited many years in exile to see you."

"Yes?" Thomas asked.

"Your father."

THE WINDS OF LIGHT CONTINUES ...

As an exiled stranger lost in the Holy Land, is Thomas of Magnus doomed to spend the rest of his life thousands of miles away from his kingdom of Magnus?

Thus, in *A City of Dreams,* startled by discovered knowledge of his past, Thomas must wander from ancient city to ancient city, now searching for any knights who survived the end of the Last Crusade.

Yet, among the ruins of Old Testament heroes, he battles more than the infidels who plague each of his journeys. Part of the fight he must win is against himself — and the woman he longs to trust. Upon his victory depends the continued survival of Magnus.

HISTORICAL NOTES

Readers may find it of interest that in the times in which the "Winds of Light" series is set, children were considered adults much earlier than now. By church law, for example, a bride had to be at least 12, a bridegroom 14. (This suggests that on occasion marriage occurred at an even earlier age!)

It is not so unusual, then, to think of Thomas of Magnus becoming accepted as a leader by the age of 15; many would already consider him a man simply because of his age. Moreover, other "men" also became leaders at remarkably young ages during those times. King Richard II, for example, was only 14 years old when he rode out to face the leaders of the Peasants' Revolt in 1381.

Chapter Three
Cathay, now known as China, was only known by legend, or by a select few travelers such as Marco Polo, who braved incredible hardship and danger to explore the Far East.

Chapter Nine
Because of widespread poverty and severity of prescribed punishment, **outlaws** were common during these times. Many faced death for crimes no more terrible than poaching the king's deer. As a result, those who escaped often banded together, and lived on the edge of desperation in hiding.

Chapter Eleven
While historians cannot establish whether an actual historical character forms a basis for the many tales collected about him, there is the possibility that the outlaw Robert who rescued Katherine was the legendary **Robin Hood.**

Several possible facts point to this. By the nineteenth century, some historians fixed Robin as one Robert Hood, who joined Thomas, Earl of Lancaster, in his 1322 uprising against Edward II. This fits with the first datable reference to Robin/Robert Hood, **which is a Yorkshire place-name,** *The Stone of Robin Hood,* cited in a document, also of the years A.D. 1322.

Coincidentally (or perhaps not coincidentally) the 38 ballads about Robin Hood place him in the forests of Sherwood, in Nottinghamshire, or **in the forests of Barndale, in Yorkshire.**

It should be noted that, as with many heroes of legend, Robin Hood has been placed in various time periods in different ballads, and that some historians identify Robin Hood with the 12th century King Richard I.

However, if the outlaw Robert Hood, so gallant to Katherine, is indeed the Robin Hood of legend, it is not improbable that in the late spring of 1313 he would reign over his band of men in the Yorkshire forests near York some nine years before some historians place him farther away in Yorkshire's Barndale forests.

Chapter Fourteen
As the Vikings lost control of the North Seas in the late 1,000s,

sea trade grew safer, and merchants began to need roomier vessels to carry larger shipments. By the year 1200, northern ship builders had developed the *cog* as the standard merchant and war vessel for the next two hundred years. One of the most dramatic improvements of the cogs was the *rudder*, a new kind of steering apparatus attached to the rear of the boat, and much stronger and more efficient for directing the boat than the oars of old.

As Thomas notes, it was much more common for the merchant ships to belong to foreign exporters of wool, such as the French, Belgiums, or Italians.

Chapter Twenty-Three

The earliest known records of **Druids** come from the 3rd century B.C., and according to the Roman general Julius Caesar (who is the principle source of today's information on Druids), this group of men studied ancient verse, natural philosophy, astronomy, and the lore of the gods. The principal doctrine of the Druids was that souls passed at death from one person to another.

Druids offered human victims for those who were in danger of death in battle or who were gravely ill. They sacrificed these victims by burning them in huge wickerwork images.

The Druids were suppressed in ancient Britain by the Roman conquerors in the first century A.D. If indeed the cult survived, it must have had to remain as secret as it was during Thomas' time.

Today, followers of the Druid cult may still be found in England worshiping the ancient runs of Stonehenge at certain times of the year.

It is difficult for historians to agree precisely on the historical **King Arthur**—while most scholars now regard Arthur's reality as probable, some wonder if he indeed existed at all—but it is commonly held that he was born around A.D. 480.

Some argue that the castle of Camelot existed at Cadbury in southern England, while others chose nearby Glastonbury. Historians do agree, however, that the legends about King Arthur (known as the Arthurian Romances) were finally put to paper by various poets in the 12th and 13th centuries, some seven centuries after the Round Table.

Merlin, legend tells us, was first an adviser to the King Uther Pendragon, King Arthur's father, then, of course, adviser to King Arthur himself. Merlin was known as the prophet of the Holy Grail—perhaps not a coincidence in light of the Druid attemps to use the Holy Grail to gain power (see *Legend of Burning Water*). Finally, Merlin was legendary as a court magician or enchanter, something not unlikely for a man with the knowledge of science available to the Druids. Through his advice to King Uther Pendragon, Merlin was responsible for the formation of the Knights of the Round Table.

Is it a remarkable coincidence that a man from York in England, named **Alcuin,** is found in the history books as the educated adviser summoned by Charles the Great (Charlemagne), the famous ruler of the Franks (Germany) in the late A.D. 700s? Alcuin helped teach all the monks and priests in Charles the Great's empire to read and write. Alcuin also introduced a new style of handwriting known as *Carolingian Minuscule*, which used small letters and was quicker and easier than writing in capitals.

Chapter Twenty-Six
The Crusades were a series of religious wars from the years A.D. 1095 (The First Crusade) to 1270 (The Eighth Crusade). These wars were organized by European powers to recover from Muslims (infidels) the Christian holy places in Palestine, especially the Holy City, Jerusalem. Many of the Crusaders believed that if

they died in battle, their souls would be taken straight to heaven.

Gradually, toward the end of the 1200s, the Muslims reconquered all the cities which had been taken from them. St. Jean d'Acre, the common destination for all ships bearing Crusaders, was the last to fall to the Muslims, and remained in Christian hands until the year A.D. 1291.